THE DEMON OF SHADOWFALL

KEVIN NAUTA

CONTENT

And now a word from the author…

Welcome to Book One of *The Shadowfall Chronicles!* As I write these lines in 2026, this book is on the eve of publication. I've always wanted to write a novel. For thirty-three years, I was busy trying to write the wrong novel and never succeeded. There's a lesson to be learned there. Sometimes you need to stop listening to your brain and start listening to your heart. This is not a story about my life. There are hints of it here and there, if you know where to look. My life is far less interesting, much quieter, and revolves around my cats. Once upon a time, I was the librarian at a very conservative Baptist church. This book would not go in that library. They would burn this book. I am no longer part of that world, and I am grateful that I left it. If you're reading this and you know me personally, you'll probably be amazed that this is the book I wrote. I'm surprised I wrote it, too.

Thank you to George Verongos for all the hard work he did editing the book and designing the beautiful cover I fell in love with immediately. I was not the easiest student in the beginning, but I learned a lot from you and could never have done this without your help. Thank you to my team of volunteer beta readers: Emily Wilson, Lyz Thelen, Amy Akers, Mark Metzger, and Brittany Steele. To my cheerleaders throughout this process—Jenn Archer, Samantha Hendricks, Stephanie Milanowski, Ruth Faraday, Brendan Bohnhorst, Stacy Jansma, and Korrine Britton, to name just a few—thank you for all your encouragement and advice. To Rose, Hannah, and everyone at New Beginnings Restaurant, where a lot of this book was written over omelets and coffee on Sunday mornings, thanks for putting up with me at my corner table. To Jennifer Johnston, who was the first to tell me I should write a book…sorry it took so long!

With that, I'll cease my prattling and turn this tale over to my characters. Hope you enjoy it!

Kevin Nauta
March 2026

I am good, but not an angel. I do sin, but I am not the devil. I am just a small girl in a big world trying to find someone to love.

—Marilyn Monroe

CHAPTER 1

My father was a failure at everything he did in life. That's a cruel thing to say about him, but it is the truth, and I believe in telling things the way they are. Mom doesn't disagree with me when I say this. She's long been rid of him and doesn't miss him one bit. She will smile at me and say, "At least I got you out of the deal." I'll smile back, hug her, and remind her he considered me a mistake. I take that personally. I will feel that way until the day I die.

Dad was the youngest son of the Rev. Eldon Brenner, pastor of Melvindale's Second Baptist Church for forty-two years. Grandpa was a bear of a man who tipped the scales at two hundred and fifty pounds with a voice that could carry to the back of the church. Eldon Brenner knew Jesus. He could tell you with complete certainty and conviction what Jesus thought of any given subject, from abortion to zoology. My grandma, Adelaide, was an equally large and noisy creature who injected herself into everyone else's business. She had come from a wealthy family with ties to Ford Motor Company and several auto parts manufacturers in Detroit.

Eldon and Adelaide had four children. Uncle Don was the oldest. He had spent most of his adult life as a missionary in Africa. He was very uncomfortable growing up in his father's shadow and made no secret of the fact that being half a world away from his father suited him just fine. They were congenial whenever he was home on furlough, raising money, but father and son never understood each other. Don was more of a pragmatist. Grandpa believed in absolutes. Aunt Deborah married a minister of a similar temperament to her father. She was submissive to a fault, never raised her voice, and—so far as I could tell—had no opinions of her own. Grandpa loved her and made a fuss over her children, but I was never very close to her or her family. Aunt Hannah was the third child. She'd left home at age eighteen and gone on to become a professor at the University of Michigan. She had been expelled from the family for her liberalism and for challenging religious dogma. According to the rest of the family, she was a God-hating, immoral child of the Devil and was never spoken of by name after that unless there was an insult attached. As a young girl, I never understood how Hannah could be all these things *and* be my aunt. Nobody explained why, either. She existed to be an object lesson on how not to live life and nothing more.

Then my father, Daniel, came along. He lived in awe of Grandpa and was forever trying to please and impress the man. Grandpa loved Dad's intelligence, fervor, and piety and groomed him as his eventual replacement at Second Baptist when he retired—something Dad knew and was eager to exploit. He went to Moody Bible Institute, the alma mater of Grandpa and Uncle Don. While he was there, he met a young woman and fellow student named Christina Powell. Her father, Michael, taught English at Moody. Her mother, Francesca, wrote books on Christian womanhood and family issues and had a busy career as a lecturer when she wasn't writing. Daniel actively pursued Christina and wanted very much to marry her. Within the college and seminary, Daniel had a good reputation and excellent grades. As heir apparent to the Second Baptist Church's pastorate, he seemed to have a promising future waiting for him. They married in 1979 after Dad graduated from seminary. Grandpa browbeat the church board into hiring Dad as an assistant pastor and began teaching him how to run the church. This would be the high point of my father's life. And it all went downhill quickly.

Dad appeared to be a very smart young man who knew his Bible and theology extremely well. What he didn't do was make people feel comfortable around him. The new Pastor Daniel Brenner seemed arrogant and self-serving at times and could be tone-deaf to the feelings of his congregants. He desperately wanted a family—or more accurately, a son of his own to dote on as his father had doted on him. He and my mother began trying right away. It was two years before she became pregnant. Dad was wildly excited and praising God loudly…until he found out he was having a daughter. Mom had a very rough pregnancy and delivery. I came into the world on May 7, 1980. Her doctors strongly urged her not to have any more children. Dad would have none of this. He valued his interpretation of God's will and power above the wisdom of those who had gone to medical school. As soon as she was able, he forced her to try to get pregnant again. One year later, she did. She nearly died in the attempt. The son Dad wanted was delivered stillborn. Both sets of grandparents pulled Dad aside and told him under no circumstances was he to get Mom pregnant again. God had spoken, and this door had closed to him. Dad accepted this and didn't try again, but he became an angry and sullen man afterwards, taking everything out on Mom and me. He was cruel, he demeaned us daily, and he wasn't above slapping or shaking us if we earned his disapproval. We never said anything, of course. He was a minister and a man of God. We were raised to be submissive, and he took full advantage of that.

He managed to hide this from the church and from the Brenner clan for a while, but his temper got the better of him just before Christmas in 1985. Dad was at church, trying to help prepare things for the yearly Christmas program. He'd asked Mom to decorate the podium in a certain way, and Mom couldn't quite grasp what he wanted her to do. She tried and failed three times. Each time, he grew more impatient with her. Finally, he lost his temper and slapped her across the face, causing her to fall. Grandma Brenner witnessed it. She pounced on him and slapped him in return and then dragged him off to the pastor's study with Mom in tow. Grandpa Brenner listened to what everyone said and fired Dad on the spot. "No man who ever would beat his wife was fit to stand in a pulpit and preach the love of Christ," Grandpa said. "You will never succeed me."

The congregation was never told the truth behind Daniel Brenner's sudden resignation as minister. Grandpa made him stand up in front of the congregation, confess to some vague sins, and vow to spend more time studying the Bible and repenting of his pride before he could become a minister again. For the next five years, Dad would try to get other ministerial jobs, only to be rebuffed at every turn. Grandpa Brenner made sure any church thinking of hiring him knew what he had done. Grandma arranged (thanks to her family connections) for him to take a job at Ford's River Rouge plant in nearby Dearborn. He was trapped on the assembly line, and he sank into anger and bitterness.

After he lost his preaching position, it was very rare for him ever to sleep in the same bed with Mom. He would eat meals with us when he got home from work, watch television, and go to bed. Throughout that time, he verbally abused Mom daily. She had been raised to be submissive and kind to her husband.

That's the way the Bible said it should be and what Grandma Powell taught her. Nothing she tried worked. The more she redoubled her efforts, the more Dad despised her. The only times he ever treated her with civility and kindness were when he was being watched at church and at family gatherings. Mom would mistake these as being a sign that he still cared about her and then try even harder to please him. This would continue for years. Divorce wasn't an option—neither the Brenner nor the Powell families approved of divorce and would have disowned any family member who tried to get one. That left my parents stuck with each other. We were also stuck with Second Baptist Church, since Grandpa and Grandma insisted our family owed its allegiance to them, and Dad never dared cross them.

CHAPTER 2

The earliest memory I have of my mom was her telling me bedtime stories. Mother was an amazing storyteller. She loved to read to me, but she just as often made up her own tales of heroes and villains and dragons and elves. Witches and wizards were also fair game, even though the church strongly disapproved of any talk about magic and witchcraft. She could make them evil, but also make them interesting, because she imagined backstories to explain why they made the choices they had. Sometimes, she even found ways to redeem them in the end. In her world, good and evil were not black and white.

Mom wrote down these stories. Every week, she'd mail them to Grandpa Powell, and Grandpa Powell kept them safe from my father. Dad wasn't above burning her writings when she displeased him. As I grew older, I started writing stories, and she mailed those to Grandpa Powell, too. Having a grandfather who taught English meant I'd get constructive criticism on my stories as part of the deal. He taught college students, but he was gifted enough to find ways to explain to a grade-schooler how to take what I knew and make it better. Mom could get away with more than I could—I wasn't allowed to write about magic. I could dream, though. One day, I would grow up and maybe be able to write about anything I wished. If I escaped, that is. I think Mom assumed she never would.

Grandpa Powell was a confusing person. He was kind to a fault and loved art, music, and writing. He bought me my first set of art pencils and a sketchbook when I was ten. He loved his daughter very much, yet he seldom intervened to improve her life or provide a means of escape. Mom said he was always afraid for his job because Eldon Brenner was on one of the school's advisory boards. Picking a fight with the Brenner family wasn't in his best interest, and he did his best to stay neutral. It didn't help that his wife was very much a proponent of Christian women being submissive to their husbands, even though she ran the Powell house with an iron fist.

I spent the early years of my childhood trying not to offend or annoy my father. Crying meant I was spanked. Being noisy meant I was spanked. Getting dirty, coming home late from a friend's house, spilling my juice—he was always there to punish me. Sometimes, he forced Mom to be the one to dole out the punishment, so that she would be complicit in the discipline. He wanted me to fear him, and it worked. I learned how to stay quiet in my room. I played with my dolls. I read my books. I wrote my stories and stayed out of his way. Those same behaviors carried on into my school years. I was the shy kid who rarely spoke, didn't seek out other children to play with, and tried to fly under the radar as much as possible. There was no question about a Brenner child going to a public school. I was enrolled in a Christian school and went to a Baptist church. I never interacted with anyone who believed in anything else. I did note that the level of belief among my peers in school varied noticeably. Everyone paid lip service to the same thing, but there were kids who were mean, told lies, cheated on tests, and were bullies. They could be punished for their misdeeds and very often were, but it didn't seem to change them any. The fact that I was Daniel Brenner's daughter earned me some pity. I was the poor child who had to deal with the legacy of a father who washed out of the ministry. The only reason I enrolled in this school was that Grandpa and Grandma Brenner paid part of the tuition; otherwise, it would have been a public school for me.

My teachers encouraged me to write and draw. Those were small things, but very important to my developing a sense of worth and purpose. I did well academically—not top of my class, but respectable enough to be noted by my teachers. When it came to religious studies, my knowledge was excellent. Still, several of my teachers through the years made remarks that I seemed unenthusiastic about my faith. My father would have given me grief about that, but he never went to parent-teacher conferences at school. He sent Mom to do it. He couldn't be bothered. Mom would only relay the positives and cover up the blemishes.

I had my father's wavy black hair, which I wore long and usually in a ponytail. From my mother, I inherited a pair of piercing blue eyes. I always wore long dresses that went to my ankles. I had my first period when I was twelve. By the time I was thirteen, my growth spurt had come and gone, and I was as tall as I was ever going to get: five feet, three inches tall. That made me shorter than my parents and both sets of grandparents. Mom said with some amusement that nature could be capricious. She was five feet, nine inches tall, and I would be looking up at her my whole life. I wasn't overly well-endowed, but boys took notice of me for the first time. Christian boys can be just as rude and annoying as their public-school counterparts. I quickly got used to wearing bulky clothing that hid my curves. It kept my father from yelling at me, too. I didn't have any choice in how my body formed, yet somehow it was my fault all the same. I assumed he thought I had a switch installed someplace where I could deflate the curves I'd been given and go back to being a little kid. Life doesn't work that way. This is the way God made me. Dad paddled me when I said that to him. I was turning into a harlot like his sister, who apparently said the same thing to Grandpa Brenner. Grandpa Brenner beat her, too. That was the way of the world, after all.

The one thing my father shared with me was the Bible. He regularly read it with me and gave me a running commentary on it, much as he would if he were still preaching. I knew it cover-to-cover thanks to Dad. I also began to realize things didn't always make sense. Some of the things we read sounded evil and horrible. When I questioned them, Dad would growl at me that I had no right to question the wisdom of Almighty God. He would explain things to excuse the bad parts and gloss over the contradictions. I learned to keep quiet about what I saw, but I didn't forget. I hid the words in my heart just as he said to do. I didn't become more devout, however. I just grew angrier.

The week before Christmas of my fourteenth year, Dad finally snapped. He'd had a bad day at work and been yelled at by his supervisor for failing to follow maintenance instructions, causing damage to the machinery. He came home and yelled at Mom, who was trying to make dinner. When she became distracted and burned the roast in the oven, Dad hit her with a closed fist… repeatedly.

I had seen this happen before. Usually, I ran away to my room and hid. Today was different, however. Today, I was done with him. I ran to the phone and called the police. They arrived at the house in three minutes. He was still hitting her when they pulled him off her, at which point he started punching them. The police dragged him off to jail then and there, and had an ambulance come and check out Mom. She'd been bruised and battered and had two black eyes. Two of her fingers were broken, and she had a couple of cracked ribs and a broken nose on top of everything else. She went to the hospital. A police officer stayed with me until Grandpa and Grandma Brenner could come to the house. We went up to the hospital together and stayed there until Mom was released.

Grandpa was furious but eventually bailed Dad out of jail. Part of his bond conditions was that he could have no contact with us, so he stayed with his parents and presumably had to listen to them browbeat him daily. Grandpa assured us that when he was finished with his son, he would behave, and none of this would happen again. We didn't believe him. Unfortunately, Mom didn't feel as if she had any say in the matter.

A couple days after Mom got out of the hospital, the phone rang at our house and she answered it. Her face suddenly became astonished. "What are you calling us for?" she exclaimed. She listened quietly to the voice on the other end for a few minutes. Then she exclaimed, "I'm not going back to him," Mom said. "I am done with this, for my own sake and the sake of my child."

The phone call continued for a few minutes. Mom grabbed a piece of paper and began scribbling down something. Then the call ended, and she hung up the phone.

I looked over at her. "Who was that?"

Mom came over and sat down beside me. "That was your Aunt Hannah."

I felt my eyebrows rise. "*The* Aunt Hannah? But why would she call us?"

Mom looked at me thoughtfully. "Someone at the police department called her and let her know what was happening. She's offering us the chance to live with her."

"But that's Aunt Hannah!" I said in disbelief. "She's a demon! Grandpa and Dad always said so."

Mom sighed. "I very much doubt that. A demon wouldn't try to rescue us. Whatever she is, she can't be any worse than your father. How do you think your dad is going to be when he gets back here? You called the police on him. I'm scared to death he'll take it out on you."

Mom had a point. "So, what do we do now?"

"Pack a suitcase. Take whatever is essential. We're leaving tonight."

We left home on the night of December 22nd with Christmas presents still under the tree. I assumed that this would be just a temporary thing and that we would be back soon. I was wrong. I never set foot in that house again.

CHAPTER 3

I'll remember my first look at Hannah Brenner's home as long as I live. To my young eyes that night, it was a huge mansion, tucked away in the countryside north of Ann Arbor on what once had been farmland. Mom's words when she drove our old Chevrolet Citation into the driveway were that she felt like the Clampetts driving into Beverly Hills. There was a foot of snow on the ground, and the house looked beautiful, snow clinging to the roof and the trees around the yard. Smoke wisped out of one of the chimneys—the house had two. We parked outside the front door and nervously walked up the front walkway to ring the doorbell. Aunt Hannah opened the door and warmly hugged my mother. "You're safe now," she said. "Stay as long as you want."

Aunt Hannah looked like no other Brenner I'd ever seen. She was forty-one years old, close to six feet tall, thin as a rail, and wore her red hair down to her waist. The Brenner family tended towards being tall, but they were all hefty folk. I wondered if she had been adopted. She came over and hugged me. "Welcome, Sarah. I am looking forward to getting to know you. Angie is excited to have someone close to her age living here, too. Erin, Tina, and Sarah are here!" It was extremely rare to hear Mom be called by her nickname. It never found favor with my father.

Erin came in from the kitchen. She was about the same height as Mom, had dark hair, and wore a tight sweater and jeans that accentuated her figure. I guessed her to be close to my mother's age. Erin had that look of someone who had seen a great deal in her life and had a lot of stories to tell. She shook Mom's hand and mine. "Erin Thompson," she said. "I run this zoo. Pleased to meet you!"

"Come! Sit down and get comfortable," Hannah said. "Is Angie doing her homework? I thought she'd be down here."

Erin laughed at the suggestion. "She's probably on the phone again. Shall I go fetch her?"

"No need. She'll come down when she's ready. We can get acquainted in the meantime. It's sad we've had no interactions all these years."

"I think I've only met you at my wedding," Mom said. "And that was briefly."

"Yes," Hannah said. "Eighteen years ago. That was weird. I was invited to the wedding, but nobody wanted me there. I left early. I am so sorry it was not a happy marriage. Daniel and I did not get along at all when we were growing up. I can't say I'm surprised by this. He was always a misogynistic little shit even then."

I couldn't help myself. I let out a little gasp. Aunt Hannah said a swear word! Mom winced a little, too.

Hannah saw our reactions and laughed. "As you can see, I am very much the person you've been told about. I do swear. I like a good glass of wine with my dinner. I do not go to church on Sundays…or any other day unless there's a wedding or a funeral." She looked at my mother and smiled. "But that's just me. Unlike my brother, I am not asking you to conform to my view of the world. All I ask of you is to treat us with the same respect we treat you. This will be a learning experience for all of us, but I think we'll work it out in time."

Mom burst into tears. Hannah gave my mother a long hug and just let her cling as she cried. I watched and marveled quietly to myself. One thing I'd been taught growing up was that true love was really something only Christians understood and could practice. Everything else was just a pale imitation of the original. That was a lie. Hannah knew love. Hannah enveloped my mother in that love, and she'd only just met her. Mom was going to heal here. Maybe this was a good place after all.

I felt a tap on my shoulder, and I turned to see who it was. Angie was standing there barefoot on the living room carpet. She was just an inch or two taller than me and wore a University of Michigan tank top and sweatpants. Her brunette hair was cut short. I never heard her enter the room.

"That was my mom a few years ago," she said. "Did he hit you, too?"

I nodded. "I could never please him."

"I know how that goes. It won't be like that here. I promise." She embraced me, and I felt myself melting into her.

I looked at her. "Why? Why is Hannah the devil? Why does my family hate her so much?"

"Because she's free and they choose not to be," Angie said.

That seemed too simple and trite an answer, yet it rang true to me somehow. I'd been enslaved to my father's anger my whole life. So had Mom. Now we were away from him, and neither of us knew how to act. We'd never been free. What do we do?

"Take Sarah's things and show her to her new room," Erin said. "I think we need some time to ourselves here."

Angie nodded knowingly, and the two of us set off.

"Fourteen, huh? You'll be going to the same school as me. That will make things much easier, and I'll make sure you have plenty of friends. It sucks being dumped in a place full of strangers."

I hadn't thought about this. My old school was far away now, and there would be no question of my returning. Suddenly, the thought of this being a temporary exile passed out of the realm of possibility.

"All our Christmas presents are back home," I mumbled to myself.

"Oh, that's no problem! We deal with these things all the time. Hannah has people who she trusts to move things for our guests when they escape on short notice. We'll get whatever you need from your house. If we can't get it, we'll replace it. Trust me, the best Christmas present you'll ever get is not having your shitty father beating you again. It's been seven years since we escaped. I don't miss my old life for a second."

Aunt Hannah's house was functionally two houses. She sometimes hosted academics for conferences and opened her home to domestic violence victims like us. The east end of the home had its own kitchen, bathroom, and laundry facilities, as well as a private entrance. Nothing fancy and not very large, but enough to give guests the option to keep to themselves and avoid interacting with the residents of the main house. Mom and I had our own rooms and our own individual bathrooms. I'd never had my own bathroom before. Mom, Dad, and I always had to share one, and that was increasingly stressful the older I got. Erin and Angie brought our bags and suitcases and helped us get settled.

In the process of unpacking my clothes, Angie could see the state of my wardrobe. I didn't have anything like what she was wearing. I didn't wear any jeans, pants, or shorts. Everything was a dress or skirt, a blouse, or a sweater. I didn't even own pajamas—only long nightdresses. When we finished, Angie flopped on my bed. I sat down beside her.

"We're close in size, I think. After you get settled and feel up to it, you and I need to raid my closet and find some stuff for you to wear that isn't a dress."

I smiled. "I think I'd like that. You're sure it won't be a problem?"

She laughed hard at that suggestion. "I have more clothes than I can use. Shopping for clothes is like a social pastime for me and my friends. I buy stuff I don't even need just because it's fun. Help yourself to what you need and look amazing wearing it."

"I'm used to hiding. I'm not supposed to be amazing. That's considered a sin. We are to be chaste and modest in our attire and humble in our demeanor."

"Let me guess. Your dad still bitched about how you looked even when you did try to be modest, right?"

I nodded uncomfortably. It was as if she could read my mind.

"That's part of the game, Sarah. It's all about control when you're an abuser. That ends today. You can be who you want now." She gave me a mischievous smile. "Not everything in my closet you're going to want to wear. I may not have the curves my mom does, but I love showing off what I do have. I think we can find enough stuff you'd feel happy wearing, though. It will be a new experience, and you may take a while to get used to it. Try it, though. At least in the comfort of your own room, if nowhere else."

"You sound like you tell people this a lot. Does Hannah help lots of women?"

"Maybe once or twice a year it happens. I've been watching how she and my mom talk to women, so I kind of know what I'm supposed to say. I've never had someone so close to my age, though. I think I'm going to like having you here. You seem nice."

"Thanks," I said. I looked down at the floor. "I've never had anyone my own age I felt I could be close to. Dad never let me bring friends over. I spent most of my time by myself. Having someone to talk to would be wonderful."

"How did you even live?" she asked me.

"Up here," I said, pointing to my head. "I wrote stories. I sketched. I thought about what I would want to do when I grew up and could escape him. I hate him. I shouldn't say that, but…"

"Why shouldn't you say that?" Her reply was sharp.

"Because I am supposed to honor him. The Bible says that."

"My dad never honored Mom or me," Angie said tersely. "He beat the shit out of us regularly. He stabbed my mother. He was a violent, drunken bum who never had a kind word for anyone. I hate him. I will hate him until I die for what he put us through."

I reached over and hugged her. "I'm supposed to honor him. But I don't think that's going to happen."

She looked at me and smiled. "Stand up."

I did. Angie walked around me, looking me over carefully. "What are you doing?"

"Sizing you up. Don't go anywhere. I think I have something I want you to try on." With that, she scampered out of the room. After five minutes, she returned with a beautiful white sundress adorned with a flower pattern and a set of pajamas. She handed me the sundress and shooed me into the bathroom.

I dutifully changed into the dress and looked at myself. The dress ended just above my knees. I'd never worn anything so short in my life! But I liked what I saw. It was a vision of what I could be. I walked out of the bathroom and looked at her. "I have knees!" I said, feeling a little self-conscious.

"And legs, even!" Angie laughed. "Mom? Hannah? Come here and tell me what you think."

The two of them were showing my mother her room next door, and they wandered over. "Nice!" Erin said. "Tina, come have a look!"

My mother came into the room and did a double-take. "It's so short."

"I feel a little naked," I admitted. "But I like it."

"The Brenners would never allow that."

Hannah smiled thoughtfully. "You never wore anything like that when you were younger?

Mom thought for a moment and then blushed a bit. "I did wear my skirts shorter when I was in high school. It was so long ago."

Hannah nodded knowingly. "That's how abusers control things, Tina. They take away pieces of who you are and replace them with visions of who they want you to be. You came here and defied him. Don't turn around and start becoming him now that you've escaped."

Erin walked up behind Mom and hugged her. "See how beautiful your daughter is? She got that from you. She has every right to shine as brightly as she can. So do you, dear. You and I both got the shit kicked out of us, and we lived. You have every right to shine just as brightly as you were meant to by the God who created you. Why would He make you beautiful and then force you to hide that beauty away? That was the voice of a man who had no control over anything except the two of you. But that is now over forever."

Memories started flooding back to my mother. She grew up in a strict Baptist household, but she went to church parties with her friends and always dressed splendidly. She loved flirting with the boys when she was a teenager. She wore lipstick and laughed uproariously and liked the Beatles and Elvis, even if she didn't advertise that fact to her parents. Daniel Brenner had taken all that away. He'd also made her forget, and she hated herself for letting it happen.

"I was beautiful once."

"And you still are. You'll be even more so when you can breathe properly and not peer over your shoulder every five minutes to see if he's behind you. When you've healed and gotten your bearings, you'll see the world as it always was. My brother caused this mess. I intend to see it fixed." Hannah nodded approvingly at me. "You wear that outfit proudly, Sarah."

"I'm jealous. I hate myself for saying it…but I'm jealous." Mom was shedding a few tears.

"Aunt Hannah, will you get her some nice clothes when she's feeling better?"

"Absolutely, I will!"

Mom broke down crying there in my room with the four of us around her, comforting her as best we could.

CHAPTER 4

Our first full day in our new home was very busy. Hannah and Erin arranged to borrow a friend's van and a couple of burly acquaintances to move whatever else we needed from our old house to here. Mom and Erin went along to supervise. I was not allowed to join them, in case Dad were to turn up unexpectedly. They returned in the afternoon with our personal effects, our Christmas presents, and even the tree itself, plus family photo albums. The rest of the furnishings, toiletries, and Dad's things were left behind. Mom called Grandpa Brenner and told him she and I had moved out. Dad could have the house. Grandpa asked her what she intended to do after this. She didn't know and told him as much. The rest of the day was spent putting all the stuff away in our new quarters.

We ate dinner together for the first time that night. Nothing fancy by any stretch of the imagination: turkey sandwiches, cream of broccoli soup, salad, and cherry pie. We gathered around the table, and I watched my mother to see what she would do. We always prayed before our meals. I doubted Aunt Hannah did. How would Mom handle it, and would Hannah get angry?

"It's a tradition for us that every time we eat dinner together, we hold hands and offer our thanks for the meal and for being able to share it with each other," Hannah said. "It isn't a prayer exactly, but it could be one. Tina, as our guest, I'll offer you the chance to lead us tonight if you wish."

Mom smiled. "I'm honored," she said. We all held hands together, and she began to speak. "Thank you for allowing us to gather here together today, and for the food we are about to share together. Thank you for giving us a moment of peace in the maelstrom that our lives have been—a chance to heal the wounds we have suffered and restore the faith in this world that has been taken from us. Grant unto our hosts the knowledge that our beliefs about them were less than true. We ask their forgiveness for our misplaced hatred of them. May we learn from each other and learn to accept each other, even when we disagree." She paused for a moment. "Finally, thank you for giving me Sarah as my daughter and companion. Thank you for her bravery in standing up to her father and seeking help when I was too weak to do so myself. May she grow to become a woman who will never let herself be bullied, and who will seek to help others arise and cast off their chains. Amen."

"Amen, indeed!" Hannah said delightfully.

"From our lips to the ears of the universe," Erin replied with a smile.

"This isn't just about Sarah," Hannah said. "May you grow to be a woman every bit as powerful as your daughter. May your light shine as brightly as it was meant to before others tried to hide it. No one is worth sacrificing that light for."

As we ate, we started chatting. "My Dad has been teaching at Moody Bible College for forty years. We never had a house like this! Does U of M pay that much better?" Mom asked.

Hannah laughed at this. "Absolutely not! I have written a few novels in my spare time that have sold a few million copies. Several of them were made into movies. I took all that money, invested it well, and built this house eight years ago. I write under the pen name Felicity Parr. I don't want my writing to disrupt my academic career, so I keep my hobby quiet."

"Mom and I write too," I said. "We've had to keep it secret for a long time, but Grandpa Powell knows and has been helping us practice. I draw, too."

Hannah's eyes lit up like a Christmas tree. "You do? We will have a lot of things to talk about then. Angie is in the art program at her high school. That gives the two of you something in common to build a friendship on."

"Have you ever been married?" I asked her.

"No," Hannah said firmly. "Never felt the need. I enjoy my life, and I'm very busy with all my projects and my teaching career. I'm very fulfilled as an adult, and I don't regret making the decision to stay single."

"Don't you get lonely?" I asked curiously.

Hannah and Erin exchanged furtive glances. "I have some very good friends who are a part of my life. If I ever get lonely, I can always call someone to help me through those times. Being single is not the same as being lonely if you build a strong support network around yourself."

Erin and Angie had been the first domestic violence victims Aunt Hannah had helped. What Hannah didn't know at the time was how gifted Erin was at running a household, scheduling appointments, and taking care of all the small details that kept Hannah from doing what she did best. They made a great team, and their friendship blossomed. Erin was now Hannah's executive assistant, agent, best friend, and companion. Erin went to school, earned a business degree, and was paid well for all the work she did. They had a wonderful vibe together. When

Erin was telling us about her life, Hannah would watch her intently and beam proudly. Angie did the same. She was a junior in high school, loved art and music, and saw Hannah as a role model.

As the meal went on, I noticed a change in my mother and me. We were used to keeping the conversation to a minimum during meals so as not to anger Dad. Here, everyone talked and laughed. It was as normal as breathing to them. We were the sick ones, and breathing this atmosphere of joy lit our spirits and loosened our tongues. Mom made the conscious decision not to be offended by the occasional casual swear words. If it didn't bother her, I wasn't going to let it bother me.

"Do you have a boyfriend?" I asked Angie innocently.

"Joey Saldana," Angie said. "He's a senior. He's a really smart guy who wants to be a mechanical engineer someday. I've been dating him since I was in ninth grade. You'll like him. He's super friendly, and he's great if you have questions about your homework. If he doesn't know the answer, my friend Kelcee does. She's so sweet! We're all great friends. She dates him, too."

I had no experience dating at all, and I didn't know much about the ins and outs of the matter. I did know one thing—or at least I thought I did. "You both can't date the same guy!"

"Says who? We both like him. We both like each other. He likes both of us. We're all happy. If other people don't understand it, that's their problem. We just do what we want and have fun."

"And no one is jealous?" Mom asked incredulously.

"What's the point?" Angie asked. "This isn't permanent. Joey's leaving for college at the end of the year. We'll have to say goodbye at some point. When the time comes, we part as friends and move on to new adventures."

"As long as my daughter follows the rules around here, she can date who she pleases," Erin said. "She's not perfect. She's kept me up a few nights since she became a teenager. All things considered, she's a better kid than I was at her age. I got pregnant in high school with her because I was stupid and dated the wrong guy. Our parents made us get married, and that just made matters worse. She's at least sensible enough to date two good people. I'm not going to argue with that."

Mom was afraid of Dad. I knew the expression she would give off when he had her backed into a corner as he shouted at her. She exhibited a different kind of fear now, one I could not understand. Angie was different. There was no denying that. She was friendly, kind, and understanding towards me. Why would Mom be afraid of her?

"How was it for you when you got kicked out by Grandpa and Grandma?" I asked.

"I think I was about your age when I began standing up to my dad," Hannah said. "There was so much I didn't know about the world then, but I thought what I was being taught wasn't about making me a better person. Weak and subservient isn't what I wanted to be. I wanted to write about things that mattered to me. I wanted to understand science, politics, and history. I wanted to love someone I was attracted to, not someone the church deemed appropriate. The more I learned about the world, the less what I was being taught at home seemed true."

"You can't dismiss everything you were taught," Mom protested.

"Very true. I look back and cringe at some of the things I said and did out of rebellion. I don't regret turning my back on my family, though. Not for one second. You have a lot to learn, both of you. You will change your mind about some things and hold fast to others. Daniel made you weak and afraid, and you can't be that way anymore, or you'll walk right back to him. If you do that, you might never get a second chance to escape. That would be a waste of a beautiful person with so much to offer the world."

"I am not going back." Mom uttered those words calmly and with a resolve I'd never heard from her.

"My dad is a total narcissist; he messed with my mom's mind during the time they were together," Angie said. "He was able to make her believe all kinds of things that weren't true and to accept the fact that everything that happened was her fault. None of it was. Not one thing. But she believed it all until one day, something in the façade he built cracked just enough for her to look through and see there was something else beyond. That's all it took. Then she saw everything clearly, and she made sure Dad would never hurt her or me again. That's you right now, I think. You just peeked through that hole to the world outside. You're not sure what to do yet. You aren't completely sure what you even see. And we can't wait to see you build yourself back up into someone amazing."

Mom was embarrassed. "I didn't do a thing. My daughter did it for me."

"Doesn't matter how it happened, Tina. Are you going to escape?" Erin reached over and put her hand on Mom's arm.

"I must."

Mom came to visit me before I went to sleep, just as she did every night. I asked her about the fearful expression I'd seen. What was she afraid of? She looked at me thoughtfully and didn't answer right away. I thought for the briefest moment that she was going to cry.

"I prayed the same prayer every night for many years," she said haltingly. "Rescue me, God. If you won't make Daniel better, at least give me a way out."

"And He did…"

"Maybe," she replied in a voice that lacked any hint of conviction. "Or maybe the demons decided to answer the call instead. What do I do when I can't tell who is good and who is evil any longer?"

"Then you be good and see which one follows you," I replied.

She kissed me gently. "I suppose that advice will work as well as any." She got up to leave and then turned back to face me. "While Hannah, Erin, and Angie are blessings to us now, they are not like us, and we should not choose to live like them. We are Christians, and we need to comport ourselves properly."

It occurred to me in that moment that they were happy, and we were the miserable ones. Might the solution be that they had a better handle on reality than we did? Mom wasn't in a place to have that discussion, so I let the matter drop.

CHAPTER 5

Our first Christmas without Dad was a happy one. Mom didn't want to bother Hannah by intruding on their Christmas Eve celebration, but Hannah wouldn't hear of it and insisted we join them.

"My niece and my sister-in-law are safe for the first Christmas in fourteen years. That's the best gift anyone could possibly give me." There were gifts for us under their Christmas tree. None of them were extravagant, and all were practical for a family starting over with very little: sheets, towels, silverware, and clothing. I also noted that their gifts to each other were very much in the same vein. For someone who was clearly very wealthy and lived in a mansion, Hannah maintained the Brenner simplicity when it came to gift-giving. The Thompsons were the same. Angie gave me the first pair of jeans I ever owned in my life, along with a South Lyon High School T-shirt, as a gift. I wore them proudly to breakfast on Christmas Morning.

It snowed on Christmas Day. I sketched the view from my window that afternoon. It was quiet in the house. Mom, Erin, and Hannah were talking together in the main house about life and our futures, and I guessed I should probably leave them alone. Angie had said at breakfast she'd be spending the afternoon with Joey and Kelcee. I hadn't noticed her leave, but I did see a car pull into the driveway as I was sketching, so I wondered if she'd returned.

A knock came at the door. "Are you decent?" Angie called out.

"Of course I'm decent. It's four in the afternoon! What kind of silly question is that?"

Angie sauntered into the room like a cat that had a high opinion of itself and flopped on my bed. "You'll learn to ask that question the longer you stay here. The last thing I want to be after a long day at school is decent." She winked at me. "You have more presents to open."

"How? There was nothing under either tree the last time I checked."

"Because Santa came back, stupid! Trust me, after all the shitty Christmases you've had, you deserve extra presents! C'mon!" With that, she dragged me out of my room and back to the main house.

That was my introduction to Joey and Kelcee. They were standing in the living room by the fireplace, each wearing a Santa suit, with a sack of presents draped over their shoulders. I had never pictured Santa wearing a red mini skirt with red flannel underwear underneath, but it was easy to see why Angie and Kelcee were such good friends. They shared the same weirdness.

"Merry Christmas, Sarah!" they shouted in unison. I didn't know what to do in the moment. I think Angie guessed I might be overwhelmed. She hugged me and then motioned the others over to do the same. I melted into their embraces. They understood what it meant to truly care about people, even if they didn't live life the way we did. Mom, Erin, and Hannah were seated in the living room, watching us, and all were smiling. Mom was crying.

I opened presents for the next half-hour. Joey gave me a coffee pot because he thought writers should always have plenty of coffee on hand while they work. He also bought me a pair of sandals. Kelcee gave me the first set of cosmetics I ever owned, plus two sets of skirts and blouses. I was also gifted with gym clothes for school, pencils and pens, a beach towel, and a bottle of suntan lotion.

"What gives with this?" I asked, holding the lotion in my hand. "It's snowing out!"

"Summer will come soon enough," Joey smiled. "There's a swimming hole on Hannah's property. We come out here regularly during the summer to sunbathe, swim, and stay on top of our homework so we don't forget everything and start the year off stupid. Especially Angie, because she's lazy and needs motivation."

"I beg your pardon! I am not lazy!" Angie bellowed. "I would rather think about other things during the summer than algebra, thank you!"

"That's why you have two honors students babysitting you. You'd spend all day at the mall if you had the choice." Kelcee smiled and nodded at Mom and Erin. "My mom is a probate court judge. She could probably pull some strings for me to get me into a good school, but I don't work that way. I want to stand on my own abilities, and I want Angie to do that, too."

After I was done, it was time for Angie and her friends to open their presents to each other, as well as Hannah and Erin's presents for them. I took the time to observe them while they were busy. Joey was a little over six feet tall, with dark hair and deeply tanned skin. I had never had a crush on anyone and didn't think I had a particular type of boy I was interested in.

Having said that, I could see why Angie thought him attractive. Kelcee seemed taller than she was at first. Once her Santa boots were off, however, she was the same height as Angie and me. She wore her red hair shoulder-length, and she had a few light freckles she hid with makeup. She appeared innocent at first glance and was certainly charming, but she had the same scent of danger to her as Angie did. It also didn't take long to figure out she was far more into Joey than Angie was. Angie and Joey were good friends. Kelcee adored Joey. I could see it in her eyes. Why were they sharing when Kelcee was so invested in him?

After the presents were opened, Joey turned to Mom and asked where I would be going to school now that I was here.

"We've been talking a bit about that," Mom said. "She can't go back to her old school. I don't have the money to pay the tuition. I guess that means she'll be going to the same school you are."

Angie hugged me excitedly. "Once Christmas is over, we'll bring our friends over to meet you. When you start school, you won't be lonely. They're going to love you as much as I do. I promise."

"I like Sarah. We'll take good care of her for you," Kelcee said.

"Do I trust them?" Mom asked Erin pointedly.

"I talk to their parents every week," she said. "You'll meet them, too, and get to know them. They are all professionals and outstanding members of the community, and they will lovingly welcome you into our parenting group."

"Obviously. The idea that these three are dating boggles my mind. That's not what I want for my daughter. I can't fathom why you allow it or even how it works."

"My parents freaked out when we told them," Joey said. "They called Erin and Kelcee's parents, and we all had a big meeting and argued a lot."

"Let's just say part of the agreement we came to was that we gotta keep it private," Angie said. "Don't flaunt it in public. Don't do anything that will make the families look bad. Don't get pregnant and don't get suspended from school."

"My parents met in a hippie commune back in the day," Kelcee said. "They did the whole free love thing before they became responsible. They think I'll grow out of it the way they did, so they're understanding. Cautious, though. Mom wants to be re-elected, and I want to get into a good college after I graduate."

Hannah smiled at Mom. "This reminds me of something a very wise woman once said: 'May we learn from each other and learn to accept each other, even when we disagree.' I believe I heard that said not too long ago." Mom recognized her own words being used against her and smirked into her chest.

"Point taken, Hannah," Mom said.

After an hour or so, Joey and Kelcee left to return to their families to open presents and celebrate, with Angie joining them. Angie hadn't returned by the time I went to bed. I did wonder as I drifted off to sleep what kind of soap opera we'd wandered into.

Mom was a bit unsettled by that conversation. I thought she might just pull us out of the house and take us back to

Melvindale. That didn't happen. What did happen was something I never expected at all. She asked Angie to help her peel a bucket of potatoes, and the two of them sat and talked for two hours one evening. I wasn't permitted to listen in. Later that night, I asked Mom what they'd discussed.

"I wanted to know how she viewed Kelcee and Joey," she said. "I wanted to understand why she thought the relationship she had was okay."

"You hate her, don't you?"

She shook her head. "No. I don't."

"How is that even possible?"

Mom laughed. "I wish I knew! She does remind me of someone I know, though."

"Satan? Madonna? Aunt Hannah?"

Mom laughed. "Actually, your Grandma Powell."

That was the last answer I would have guessed. "Grandma Powell would never **ever** share Grandpa with another woman.

"You are most certainly correct in that! Grandma Powell is a good Christian woman to her core. But she also loves sex. She gives lectures and teaches women how to enjoy their sexuality with their husbands while being a devout Christian woman. In her world, Christians should have the best sex."

"I never knew she did that!"

"I wasn't going to tell you that until you were older, but I think we are both going to be growing up a bit around here. Grandma Powell would have some choice words for Angie, but they'd compare notes afterwards. I pray Angie finds someone who loves her for who she truly is. After talking to her, I can honestly say Angie's not a bad person. Misled, certainly. Confused, probably. She's got a big heart. She certainly cares a lot for you. I don't want to see you become her, but I think you two could be good for each other."

This totally caught me off guard. "Thank you for talking to her," I said. "Dad would never have tried to understand her."

"I want to understand why she is who she is. Hannah, Erin, and I have talked about things, too. I'm getting to know them. If we're going to live here, we're going to have to learn how to get along with each other."

The fact that she could say that put her light-years ahead of my father and Grandpa Brenner in my book.

CHAPTER 6

Aunt Hannah shared Grandpa's opinion that there were no free rides in life. We were not paying rent, but we were expected to help around the house by cooking, cleaning a little, and taking care of everything in our suite of rooms. Mom enjoyed cooking when she was first married. With him gone, she quickly rediscovered her love for the culinary arts, and our new hosts quickly became spoiled. Erin was a fine cook, but her time was spread thin on other things. Mom had the time Erin didn't, and the kitchen soon became her territory.

I had the run of the house and did a lot of exploring. The main floor was home to Hannah and Erin's offices, the kitchen and dining room, the living room, and a parlor for greeting guests. There was also a music room with a grand piano and a huge stereo system, as well as a changing room next to the patio where the hot tub was located. The bedrooms were on the second floor, along with a library, a large bathroom featuring a jacuzzi, and a fitness room with weights and exercise equipment. The basement was primarily used for storage, but also housed an extensive wine cellar and a walk-in vault for storing valuables. The house had a three-stall garage and an old barn on the property. Most of the rooms in our wing were lightly furnished apart from the ones we were occupying. If needed, Erin would quickly add items from storage to make them ready for guests. Mom had commandeered one room to use as a chapel where she could pray. There was absolutely nothing stopping her from praying in her own room or anywhere else she chose. Her chapel was simply her way of staking out a claim that whatever mischief went on in the main house, God was welcome in our quarters. Hannah was not in the least bit bothered by this and even helped Mom furnish the room. Erin had a good laugh at Hannah helping hang a crucifix on the wall, and showed up with a fire extinguisher in case Hannah burst into flames. She did not, and Mom hugged her afterwards.

I loved my new home, and I loved being around Aunt Hannah. She was like a stiff breeze blowing through the corridors of my life, airing out the musty passages filled with anger and sadness. She was busy writing her next novel, *Belladonna,* about a female who poisons random people she meets for sport and the police detectives trying to solve the murder spree. She would talk to me as she wrote, discussing any number of things that came to mind. The more I spoke with her, the more I found I liked and empathized with her.

"A lot of women I've met coming out of domestic violence situations are very withdrawn and afraid of reaching out to people," she said. "Your mom is like that in a lot of ways, though I see a little spark trying to ignite in her since you arrived. But you, Sarah… You're different. You seem to want to throw off the weight you bore in that house and be more yourself as soon as possible. Just make sure you are comfortable with wherever finding yourself takes you. Diving into anything before you're ready is just as troublesome as being afraid to dive in at all."

"I hated my father," I said. "I hated having to be quiet and not say what I felt. I wanted to write and tell stories and ask questions and be silly. I've been waiting all this time to get the chance to be myself. Do you think I wouldn't take it now that it's here?"

Hannah smiled. "I see a little of myself in you, too. Grandpa gave me more than my share of spankings, trying to get the wicked out of me, and it never worked. The older I got, the less afraid of him I became. Time was on my side. I could leave when I was older. Grandpa and Grandma couldn't wait to kick me out, and I swore at them on my way out the door. It was juvenile and petty, but I've never regretted it. You should probably sit down and write out some notes to deliver in court when the judge sentences him, in case he asks your opinion on what to do with him."

"I was never as brave as you were," I said. "Not being a problem made it easier for Mom to be safe. I can let go of that now." I paused and thought of my mother's warning. "Mom says we shouldn't live the way you do. But I'm not sure I agree."

Hannah raised an eyebrow. "She's afraid. If you've been asleep and wake up to a bright light in your face, your eyes are overwhelmed at first. It takes a little while for your vision to adjust and for you to see clearly. That's where she is right now. You need to give her a little grace and time to figure out what's right for her in her new life. That said, you have every right to pursue the world on your own terms, and I'll have your back if that's what you decide to do. You are not beholden to your mother for the rest of your life. You can be who you want to be, even if that makes her uncomfortable. The difference between Tina and your Grandma Brenner is that Tina will still love you no matter what. My mom will never love me as I am now, and I will never change to gain her love back, or anyone else's, for that matter. Just keep that in your pocket when you're angry with your mom for not understanding you. That woman went through hell doing the best she could to be a good mother to you. You two love each other. Cherish that."

In the Bible, there's a story where Jesus meets a Samaritan woman at the town well and wins her as a convert by his calm demeanor and his willingness to meet her where she was—a sinner of a tribe the Jewish people considered apostates. Hannah was like that in reverse. She knew my heart and loved me as a person, even if I came from a tradition that despised everything she stood for.

That Samaritan woman converted many of her fellow villagers to follow Jesus because of her simple testimony. I wondered if one day, I would switch sides for similar reasons. The thought should have terrified me. Grandpa preached so his congregation would fear even the slightest sin as an avenue for Satan to take control of us. This is the devil's house, and I'm already admiring the pitchforks.

There was one room in the house I had not seen: Angie's bedroom. She visited my room all the time but never asked me to come to her room. At first, I assumed it must be because it was messy. The more I watched her habits, however, the less likely it seemed she was a slob. What was there that she didn't want me to see? When she said one night that she had some clothes for me to try on, I came out and asked her. "Why can't I see your room?"

"Your mom said it wouldn't be a good idea yet."

"You think maybe I should be the judge of that? I'm in high school. What could you have that I shouldn't see?"

"A lot of things, if you know where to look," she replied. "You're sheltered. I don't want to make you grow up any faster than you have to."

"I've been in a bubble for fourteen years! When does she plan on letting me out?"

"Maybe never. She's got her own chapel now. Weird."

I sighed. "Mom needs that right now. I don't use it. If I need to pray, I'll pray in my own bed. It's more comfortable anyway."

"I can bring the stuff to your room. It's no big deal. When we know each other better, maybe they'll be more accepting of our friendship."

"I can decide for myself who I want to be friends with! I don't need her fucking help!" I was angry when I said that. I spat out the words in disgust. Then I saw Angie break down giggling, and I had no idea what was funny. Then it dawned on me. "I just swore, didn't I?"

Through the giggling, Angie managed to stammer out a reply. "You did!"

"My dad never even swore at us all the times he was shouting and hitting us." I was genuinely embarrassed.

"C'mon. You're ready," Angie said, still laughing. "We can talk through the rest."

We walked upstairs to her room, and she opened the door. I walked in and looked around. It seemed like a normal room. There was a desk, a dresser for clothes, a bed…a very large bed. Three pillows? I jumped on the bed and sprawled out. "Big enough for three?"

"Yeah. You figured it out."

"Nobody did that back at the Christian school I went to."

Angie chuckled. "That does not surprise me. Nobody else does that at my school. We're the only polyamorous relationship I know of."

"Polyamorous? That's just a threesome with a PhD, right?"

Angie gave me a playful whack. "No, silly. Anybody can have a threesome. All you need is three people. You fuck, and then it's over. A polyamorous relationship is a committed relationship between more than two people. The three of us can sleep over and not have sex at all. We do that sometimes. If one of us isn't in the mood, the other two can have sex, and nobody gets jealous. But we do have threesomes together. We love each other. Why shouldn't we? We're not letting it get in the way of our schoolwork. We're careful. Kelcee and I are on the pill. Joey uses condoms." She sat down on the bed beside me. "Your mom and I had a long talk about this. She doesn't want me to get you involved, but this is who I am, and you need to know the truth about me. Do you hate me now?"

"I'm supposed to. Everything I've been taught tells me I should." I took a deep breath. My heart was telling me one thing while my brain was screaming something different at me. I had a decision to make. One that would change my future one way or the other…and in that moment, I made my choice. I sat up and embraced Angie from behind. "We are friends. This changes nothing."

"But your faith. Your beliefs…"

"I'll deal with those on my own terms. What else do you have to confess? Let me know it all."

"So much for protecting you," she laughed. "I like getting drunk and high. I like sunbathing naked and skinny dipping in the pond."

I sighed and lay back down on the bed. "I suppose there's no chance I could change your mind and get you to repent?"

"Why would I do that? I like sex and wine coolers! And tickling annoying little girls!" She promptly pounced on me, and we wound up in a heap on the bed, laughing hysterically. "If you ever tell your mother we had this conversation…"

"Not going to happen!"

"Do you mind if I braid your hair?" Angie asked as we lay together on the bed. "I remember doing this with Kelcee all the time when we were your age."

"Not at all." I sat cross-legged on the bed, and she set to work.

"I thought for sure you'd run out of here," she said quietly.

"I thought about it," I admitted. "Part of me is scared."

"Only part?"

"I have questions," I said. "This makes me curious about how you live."

"I don't mind people asking those questions. It's the ones who judge without knowing the answers that piss me off."

"Which do you like better: boys or girls?"

"Women. I like the connection I have—it seems deeper and more intimate than with guys. Women understand me better. Joey is a sweetheart, and he tries his best, but I've known Kelcee since I moved here, and she's my best friend."

"How did you decide this was even a way you could live?"

"Hannah has friends she hangs with. When she needs companionship and sex, she has safe people to be with—men and women. She just doesn't need that in her life to the degree I do."

"Do your mom and Hannah…um…"

"Have sex? Yes. Not all the time. When they need each other, they just ask."

"Would you ever ask anyone else?"

"Is that an offer?" she chuckled.

"No! I was just seeing how your relationship worked!"

"I've thought about it, sure. But I've never done it. That person would have to be incredibly special to me and someone my partners would approve of."

"I grew up hearing people tell me all the time how bad everything in the world was. The wages of sin is death. People who do drugs and drink get addicted. People who have sex when they aren't supposed to get diseases and get pregnant, and all live sad lives. You don't worry about that?"

Angie didn't say anything at first. I wondered if I offended her. She kept braiding my hair, however, and her touch remained just as gentle.

"I know someone in my art class who chews gum all the time. She can't function without it, I swear. People can be addicted to anything, even religion. I love sex. I love booze and pot. Do I do them all the time? Of course not! I try to maintain balance in my life to achieve all the things I want. I don't need to be saved from anything and then be enslaved to something else. I like who I am now."

"Grandpa would say you are using those things to cover the pain you feel in your own life from growing up in an abusive environment and not having a good father figure."

"Maybe a bit," Angie admitted. "But I would say I am learning how to accept myself and all the good things the world has to offer and not wallow in self-pity. He's angry that I don't want to buy what he's selling. Maybe that cure works for other people, but it doesn't sound healthy to me. That probably sounds like I'm shitting all over your beliefs, doesn't it?"

"Yes," I said. "I'd be angry if I held those beliefs to heart like Dad and Grandpa do. But I don't. I've always had to hide what I felt."

She stopped braiding my hair and put her arms around my waist, drawing me closer to her. "You will never have to do that in this house. I don't care if you're a Christian or not. I just want you to be happy. "

I did get that pile of clothes later in the evening. I tried on skirts of various lengths, jeans and capri pants, sweaters and shirts, gym shorts and sweatpants for school, a gorgeous silk bathrobe, and a one-piece swimsuit. I marveled at my appearance in the mirror. I looked good, showing a little leg and accentuating my curves. I wasn't evil. I was the same person I always was and the way God made me. I didn't have to hide anymore. I would still have to learn to deal with leering boys, but it seemed easier knowing I would have people watching over me.

I showed off some of the clothes to my mother, who gave me her glowing approval. "Hannah and Erin want to update my wardrobe, too," she said. "I think I'll let them."

This was news! "You threw a fit the first time you saw me in Angie's clothes!" I teased her.

Mom sighed and shrugged. "Yes, I did. Having been here for a while, I admire Erin's fashion sense. She's always so professional when she's working, and I'd like to feel that confident going forward."

Erin clapped her hands gleefully. "Whenever you're ready, we can hit the stores. Find your style and embrace it. That's part of healing."

That may seem a tiny step, but moving at all was a new thing for Mom. Baby steps breed confidence. One day, she'll put my father to shame.

CHAPTER 7

I was enrolled in South Lyon High School three days after Christmas. My transcripts would be sent from my old school, and I'd be allowed to start right away once the break ended. I would have algebra, American history, biology, choir, art, and English as my classes. Mom also had some preliminary talks with a lawyer friend of Hannah's about initiating divorce proceedings against my father.

The issue of divorce was one Mom struggled with mightily, coming as we did from a church that refused to accept divorce except in rare conditions. Domestic abuse could be one of those exceptions, but Grandpa Brenner had preached on this subject before, and he urged forgiveness and counseling to try to keep the family together. Hannah guessed that he would be even less likely to countenance a divorce in this situation because of the embarrassment it would bring to him and his family. Daniel hadn't responded to counseling before. There was little chance he'd grown any wiser in the years since he'd been fired by the church. Mom wept bitterly when she made up her mind to go ahead and end her marriage.

I walked into her bedroom that night and hugged her. "I'm proud of you," I said. "I know it wasn't easy."

She smiled bravely at me through the tears. "I was so excited on my wedding day. I loved your father so much. We had so many dreams."

"You couldn't know how it would turn out," I said. "He fooled a lot of people along the way." I paused as a thought occurred to me. "Do Grandma and Grandpa Brenner know we're here?"

"No," she said. "I'm communicating with them and my parents through a third party. They know we're okay and that we've moved out. We'll tell them more when we can."

"God, it sucks. Why are we on the run and Dad's at home eating ice cream and telling everyone it's our fault?"

"Your father's in court soon. We might have to go back and testify. I'm not sure yet. Depends on whether he accepts a plea deal or wants the case to go to trial."

"Do I have to say anything, or will it just be you talking?"

"I think you have every right to say what's on your heart. It won't be easy saying it in front of him. We were afraid of him for so long; speaking out with him there is going to be terrifying. I need to do it, though, otherwise I'll just stay a victim for the rest of my life. That's not what I want. I will be praying for courage, but I intend to be heard."

"I want the judge to hear me," I said. "Dad needs to know what he did was wrong and that we're never going to let him hurt us again."

Mom nodded through her tears. I could understand why. He still came to us in our dreams and screamed at us. His appearances were fewer now, but he would always live in our heads and creep out at odd moments. Recovery is learning how to manage those times and not letting them define the future. Hannah had gotten both of us to see a therapist and start learning how to cope with what we'd been through. Dad said psychiatry was another of the devil's tools. He hated being sent to see a marriage counselor by his father. It had radicalized him even more into his misogyny. It made me want to send Satan a thank-you card for giving us another resource to escape the world we had to live in. The "dark" side seemed brighter and brighter with every passing day.

***

On the morning of New Year's Eve, I was sitting in my room writing when Mom came in. "You have some friends here to see you," she said with a smile. Angie told me she was working on getting me some minders to help me get adjusted to school. I followed Mom out of the room and out of our wing to the living room of the main quarters.

"Welcome to South Lyon High!" came a chorus of voices. Angie was there, and so were Kelcee and Joey. Eight other students had joined them, holding up a huge banner that read *"Welcome, Sarah!"* I started bawling on the spot and ran over to greet my new friends.

I expected Angie or Joey to introduce everyone to me, but they stepped aside and allowed a blonde to step forward and handle things. She was taller than all the other girls in the group and carried herself with an air of importance.

"Hi, Sarah. I'm Melanie Bingham, freshman class president. Kelcee's my big sister, and she asked me to help get you settled. We have all your textbooks, so you'll be able to fit in on your first day. You are invited to join our study sessions after class. We have some of the best students in the school

51

ready to help you. We also have a few weirdoes who will love you to death, too. You've already met three of them."

Angie shrugged. "Believe it or not, I don't have a lot of friends. Being different means paying a price in terms of popularity. Joey could have been the senior class president if he wanted to. All he had to do was ditch us." She and Kelcee leaned over and kissed him.

"He wouldn't do it," Kelcee said, looking at him proudly.

"Not a chance," he agreed even more proudly.

"I don't pretend to understand my sister sometimes, but I love her to death," Melanie replied. "If no one else will stand with her, I will. I found a few friends who think the way I do, and we adopted my sister and her partners into our group. The only way this group of friends could be better is if you'd join us."

"I'd be honored!" I said excitedly.

"You'll be in English, choir, and American history with me," Melanie added. "Everyone, come and introduce yourselves!"

The first to answer her summons was a giant. "Chad Ellis," he said awkwardly. "I'm on the basketball team."

"I've never met anyone as tall as you!" I exclaimed. "Are you any good?"

"Not bad," he said quietly.

"C'mon, you can sell yourself better than that! You've had pro scouts watching you since you were in junior high!" A perky, dark-skinned girl sidled up next to him. She had a distinctly African accent, the sort I recognized from the missionary movies Uncle Don would play in church. "I'm Dee Turner, Chad's girlfriend. He's Godzilla on the basketball court, and they call me the Beast on the volleyball court. You're in my biology class along with Chad."

"You're in my English class, too," Chad added. "Melanie told me to make sure you knew to look out for me."

I giggled and hugged him. "I will do that. How long have you two been going out?"

"Seventh grade," Dee said proudly. "Thank God I grew a bit since then. I needed a stepladder to hug him on our first date!" She smiled at Chad, and he broke his awkward demeanor to meet it with a warm grin of his own.

Next to greet me was a slender Asian girl. "I'm Yuki Hasegawa, freshman class treasurer. I play clarinet in the marching band, love anime, and I help Melanie keep this bunch of delinquents in line. I'll be in your English and algebra classes. I speak three languages and can swear in eleven others."

"I've only just learned to swear in one," I grinned.

"I'd better not catch you swearing in any language, young lady!" I heard from the other side of the room.

"Sorry, Mom!"

"Mine hate it when I swear, too!" Yuki chuckled. She turned and grabbed the boy standing beside her. "This is our class vice-president, Dan Spillner. Mel, Dan, and I all have had perfect grades since we started junior high together."

"We are quite the group. All three of us study together, and our goal is to be valedictorians together, since we're all good friends," Dan added. "I'll be in choir and biology with you. I love acting. I do plays and commercials and model a bit for advertisements.”

“Do you want to become an actor when you’re older?” I asked.

“Nah, I’m thinking law school. So’s Melanie.”

“Hey, Dan! We get Sarah in choir together!” The voice came from a young man with curly brown hair and a lilting, almost angelic falsetto. “I’m Brian Phillips. I’m also in your history class.”

At that moment, a manic bundle of energy bounced over and hugged us both. “Lucy Swinton! You’re in my art class! I can’t wait for us to hang out! I love cats and poetry. I also love annoying Mel and Yuki. They’re so proper!”

Lucy was a sight to behold. She had long black hair tied in a ponytail and piercing dark eyes. She conspicuously wore both a pentagram and a crucifix around her neck. She was born to cause mischief, and she reveled in it. I suddenly found myself adoring her.

Melanie sidled over to us. “We love Lucy. We’re not always sure why, however.”

“I hear you’re the good girl,” she said with a smile. “I’m the angel of darkness. I will oversee the corrupting of your soul.”

“I’m Sarah. Distressingly good, sheltered, and naïve.” I smiled back at her. “And you’re a liar. If you weren’t an angel, you wouldn’t be here.”

Melanie started laughing. “Lucy, quit being a shit. We all know you’re soft as a marshmallow. If anyone’s going to corrupt Sarah, it will be Angie and my sister.”

"You only think you know me. I'm really a witch, and I like to cast spells to befuddle silly women like you, Melanie!" Lucy gave her a theatrical finger-wiggle.

"Would you cast a spell on me?" I asked her innocently. "Do I need to pray for protection against you tonight?"

She whispered her answer in my ear. "Wouldn't you like to know?"

"Yes, I would," I whispered back. "I think I can take you."

"Do it." She stared at me and stretched out her arm in my direction.

"Bitch, quit it! Sixty seconds and you're already tryin' to cast a spell on the poor girl!" Dee was laughing at us. Lucy flipped her off.

I jumped Lucy and started tickling her, shouting, "The power of Christ compels you, demon!" Lucy made a show of trying to tickle me back before she playfully submitted.

"You are totally going to be one of us, Sarah!" Melanie said proudly. "Robert, you're the last one. Get over here and say hello while I drag this lunatic out and throw her in the snow."

Robert approached and carefully looked me over. He didn't say anything at first, and then he smiled. Dear God, he had a beautiful smile. "I'm Robert Hill. I apologize in advance. My dad's going to be your biology teacher. He likes to tell jokes…and he's pretty bad at it."

I giggled. "Thanks for the warning. What should I know about you?"

"I love biology and astronomy, listening to my dad's old records, swimming and canoeing, and I'll be in your history and English classes. I don't cast any spells, though."

"Good to know," I smiled.

"I like your braids," he said, shyly gazing down. I knew from the way he looked at me that he was saying exactly what he felt, and that telling me that might have been the scariest thing he had ever done in his life.

"I'll make sure I wear them for you now and then." As soon as the words left my mouth, I was shocked. What was I thinking, leading him on like that?

"I'd like that." That smile again. I felt myself melting.

Erin announced that there were snacks in the kitchen, and everyone promptly headed off to stuff their faces. Robert turned back to look at me before he left and let loose that smile once more. Troublesome rogue! I'll have to keep my eye on him.

CHAPTER 8

I said a quiet prayer of gratitude when my mother dropped Angie and me off at the front gate of my new school. There would be no terror of trying to find my locker or getting lost on the way to class. My friends had planned everything out to make my first day at South Lyon High School as easy as possible. I had my books. I completed my assignments, and I turned them in before the start of each class. I just wanted to fit in and not stand out too much. I would leave that to the livelier students in my friend group. The fact that I was ready to go from the moment I introduced myself didn't go unnoticed by my teachers, either. Transfer students arriving in the middle of a semester aren't unusual, but they are an inconvenience. That my friends and I had done so much to minimize the extra work they would have to do was greatly appreciated.

Most days after school, our group would meet for study sessions at each other's houses. Melanie set up a schedule each month so our parents knew where we would be on any given day. The sessions were not exclusive to our group, either. Often, other kids would join us—classmates who needed help were always welcome. Everyone's parents knew each other, and they developed their own social network. Mom soon found herself with a whole new set of friends outside of the mansion. Brian's parents were active in the school's parent-teacher organization and quickly recruited her to join them. That gave her an added sense of purpose and the peace of mind that I wasn't out there on my own. Every one of us was being watched over and guided by teachers and parents who weren't afraid to let the others know if something was amiss. Those same teachers and parents watched over each other with the same care and tenderness. We had always relied on the church to be our community. Now we had another support group we could fall back on. Every day, Mom and I grew a little bit stronger.

My father took a plea bargain. In exchange for the felony charges of assaulting a police officer being reduced to a misdemeanor, he would enter a guilty plea. He would have to do less jail time that way. He'd be on probation for a year or two after that and wasn't allowed to have contact with us. On the day of his sentencing, I took the day off from school. Hannah thought about going, but decided against it, lest Dad figure out she was involved and guess where we were staying. Grandpa and Grandma Brenner were in the gallery, along with Chandra Fanning, Mom's divorce lawyer, compliments of Aunt Hannah. Mom and I sat with the prosecutor. We'd been asked to have statements ready to read to the judge at sentencing. Since Hannah had already put the thought in my head, I'd been pondering what I'd say to him if I ever got the chance. Writing out a statement without swearing and vitriol was difficult but cathartic, even though I had no idea what catharsis was then.

Dad listened to the proceedings in silence. He only spoke when he was required to and let his attorney handle the rest. The judge asked my mother if she wanted to say anything. Mom did.

"Your honor, I endured many years of abuse at my husband's hands," she said. "He seldom let a day pass without belittling my daughter and me. I am glad he will be facing time in jail to reflect on his actions. I wish it were longer. I will not return to him. I wish him well and hope he can become a better person in the future."

I heard murmurs from behind me. Grandpa and Grandma weren't happy with this bit of news. Dad never looked at her as she spoke. The judge asked me if I had a statement, and I nodded. I stared contemptuously at the man who had made my life hell for fourteen years.

"My father wanted a son," I said. "He never wanted me. He told me that to my face many times, especially when he was angry with me, growing up. I was stupid. I was a failure, not only in his eyes, but in the eyes of God himself." I had to pause. I was starting to cry. Mom hugged me. Dad was furious. I took a deep breath, gathered my wits, and continued. "I've learned something in the last few days. I'm not a failure. I have new friends who care about me. I can see my mother starting to heal. I wake up every day excited to be alive now. I'm not as good a person as my mother. I can't forgive you, Dad. I hope I never see you again." I sat down.

"You're just like Hannah," Dad said. "Worthless bitch!"

His attorney looked horrified. He knew my father had just made his situation much worse.

"Mr. Brenner," the judge said thoughtfully. "I think you are not the least bit sorry for what you did." Dad was only supposed to spend thirty days in jail. He wound up with ninety instead.

After the hearing was over, Grandpa made his way over to Mom. "My son is an idiot," he said. "I wish we had known."

"It's over now," Mom said. "You can deal with him."

"What are your plans now? Where are you living? Once he's out, all of you need to be in counseling so we can get the family back together. It's what God would want."

"That is not what I want," Mom said. "The days of the Brenner family dictating how my daughter and I live our lives are over. I can read the Bible as well as you. I'll draw my own conclusions on what I must do going forward."

Grandpa did not like to be addressed so curtly. He demanded respect, and he blocked Mom from leaving the courtroom.

"Sir, if you don't step aside and let my client leave, I'm going to have the bailiff move you," Chandra said in a loud voice. The bailiff heard that and sauntered over to see what the commotion was about. Grandpa knew when he was losing and let us through.

On the way to the parking garage, Mom turned to Chandra. "Do you think I could get my maiden name back? I think I've had quite enough of being a Brenner."

"Me too!" I replied.

"I can do that!" she said with a smile. While it would take a while to complete all the legal formalities, from that day on, I proudly handed in my school assignments as "Sarah Powell."

***

We were having dinner together when I asked Mom if she'd ever questioned the church or God when she was younger. Mom shook her head. "Never. Everything was set in stone, and there was nothing to be questioned."

"You seem to be questioning a lot of things right now," I said.

"Questioning, struggling, praying... I'm doing all those things. There's so much I don't understand about the world. It feels like I've been asleep for thirty-eight years and the whole universe has changed. Hannah and Erin are helping explain things. I have some serious disagreements with them on some matters, but I am trying to understand them as they are trying to understand me."

"I went through that process too when I was younger," Hannah said. "You've made an amazing start in rebuilding her life, Tina. Working through your beliefs—deciding what you want to keep and what doesn't suit you any longer. That takes a lot of time and reflection. Honestly, it is a lifelong process. The more we learn, the more we grow. The more we grow, the more we question and reevaluate old beliefs."

"There will always be non-negotiable points of faith for me, I think," Mom added. "That said, I've certainly recognized a lot of stuff we were fed through the years doesn't fit that category. That I can let go of without too much difficulty."

Knowing my mother as well as I did, I could guess what things were troubling her. If the Bible said something happened, it had to have happened. If the Bible said something was wrong, it had to be wrong. We had that mantra drummed into us so much that it permeated every part of our psyches. To some extent, I was still struggling with that as well. I had just seen too much of "good" and "moral" people behaving wickedly (or looking the other way while others did) to retain an unquestioning trust in the system I grew up in. Angie seemed to possess more love and wisdom than my father ever had. Hers was a different strand of morality and character. I wanted to understand it.

CHAPTER 9

Valentine's Day was three weeks away, and with it came the South Lyon High Sweetheart Swirl. Students were already asking each other out in mid-January. Dancing wasn't allowed at my old school, so I wasn't planning on going because I assumed Mom wouldn't consider the idea. We were all together over at Melanie's house studying one evening. Mom was there with us. She'd come along to talk about some PTA stuff with the Binghams, or so she'd said. It seemed to me she was still trying to work out why nobody was bothering to intervene in Angie's polyamorous relationship and was trying to understand other parents' rationales for letting it go on. That was none of my concern.

"Sarah," called Lucy as she and Brian caught up. "Are you going to the Swirl?"

"No. At my old school, we weren't allowed to dance. The church forbids it, and I don't think my mom would even let me."

"That's stupid! You need to ask your mom, or I'm going to ask for you."

"Even if she did say yes, I don't know how to dance!" I protested.

"We could teach her," Brian said.

"I'm game," Lucy replied. She smiled wickedly at the thought. "I already know someone who is dying to ask you to be his date."

"What? Who?"

"I'm not telling. If you aren't going, I'll hook him up with someone else. Like Melanie. She'd go if he asked."

"I might indeed!" Melanie said with a grin as we met her in the hall. Clearly, she was in on the secret. "As soon as we're done with our homework, let's all teach Sarah a few moves, and she'll fit right in."

She meant it. As soon as we were finished, she scurried off and asked her father to help rearrange the furniture in the basement so we would have room to practice. Mr. Bingham popped into the room.

"Did you want to learn how to dance?" he asked. "Or is the mob trying to twist your arm?"

"Dad! You're not helping!" Melanie protested.

"I don't know if it is something I'd like," I said. "But I at least want to try it and see if I'm comfortable with it."

"A fair answer," he said. "Mr. Collins did ask your mother if she would help chaperone the dance with the PTA. She said she'd never been to a dance and thought she'd feel out of place. So maybe it would be easier if you both went. And you two are free to leave early if you decide to."

"It's just a dance. You go, you wave your arms around a little, move your feet, drink some punch, and go home," Lucy said.

"Maybe that's what it is to you," Mr. Bingham replied. "Sarah and her mom come from a place where not only is dancing wrong, but even wanting to dance is something their religion deemed punishable. Am I right?"

I nodded, feeling a little embarrassed, but also relieved to have left that all behind. I just needed to be gently pushed over the line.

"But that's awful!" Dee said. "Our family goes to church every Sunday, and dance is a part of it. Our culture views dancing as a form of worship and a way of expressing emotions. Not being able to express yourself…how did you live?"

"Quietly," I said. "I don't want to live that way anymore."

Even though my new friends had a basic understanding of what my life used to be like, I don't think some of them realized how strict and controlled it was.

"So, it's like that movie *Footloose*, only for real?" Yuki asked.

"Except she couldn't listen to the radio either," Angie said tartly. "Or watch half of the stuff we did on television."

"But that's crazy!" Yuki said in disbelief.

"I'm not crazy, though. I'm just way behind the rest of the world," I said.

"And the thing you are all thinking right now is how much you want to help her catch up," Mr. Bingham said. "And you simply can't do it all at once, no matter how much you care about her. I suggest not overwhelming her and just take it a little at a time. Sarah will set her own pace, but the first thing we need to do is ask Sarah's mother if she can go. Nothing else can happen unless she says yes."

Soon after Mr. Bingham returned to the living room, where his wife and my mom were visiting, he reappeared in the doorway with Mrs. Bingham and Mom in tow. "Sarah, I believe you have a question you want to ask your mother."

I didn't expect this to happen right then, but I steadied myself and took a deep breath. "Yes. Can I go to Sweetheart Swirl, Mom?"

"I think that would be okay. I'll be there chaperoning. I don't see why not."

I ran over and hugged her.

"That was a lot of drama over nothing," Lucy chuckled.

"I'm excited and a little scared to hear what kind of music teenagers listen to," Mom said, half joking. It will be an opportunity to see what normal kids do and give me a little window into the world we've been kept from."

"Yeah, your mom might be a little behind the times—wait, what were you guys dancing to back when you were our age?" Lucy asked the adults.

"The Beatles and Elvis were huge back then," Mom said. "That's who we always heard were corrupting the youth of America in sermons."

Everyone had a good laugh, and it was nice to see Mom shine.

The rest of that night was amazing. Once the furniture was cleared away, Melanie threw on a mix tape. I did not become the world's greatest dancer, and I didn't care. I just loved the freedom it gave me to express myself. I also understood that very thing was one of the reasons why our church hated rock music and dancing so much. Expressing ourselves was sinful. Showing the world my excitement, vulnerability, sexuality, and anger was considered pride and hubris, not the proper humility and Christ-centeredness a young saint should have. Except I wasn't a saint anymore. I was lighting that part of my life on fire and watching it burn, swaying to the music and clapping my hands in time.

****

Mom and I drove home together with the radio playing quietly in the background.

"So, what did you learn from talking with the Binghams?" I asked.

"This and that," she replied. "Some of it is private."

"That bad?"

"Different. Grandpa would call it bad, but he's not here, and I'm not telling him. They have their own experiences they fall back on when raising their children. They believe their kids to have good instincts, and they trust them to make good decisions. I mean, the two oldest have already graduated from medical school. Melanie wants to be a lawyer like her mother. Kelcee wants to be an engineer."

"And Kelcee's relationship with Angie and Joey?"

"Is not what they'd prefer, but it isn't detrimental to her present success. As long as they are all doing well and are not harming anyone, Bruce and Caroline are happy to let them do their own thing. They doubt the relationship will prove sustainable over time, but the kids will figure that out on their own and make that decision themselves. That's how you learn to be adults in their world—make decisions, explore the world, and deal with the consequences."

"Sounds reasonable to me," I said.

Mom stared out into the darkness. "That's not how we do things. We follow the rules God has put before us. God's word is sovereign, a father's word is law, and a child's function is to obey. But look where that got us."

I couldn't tell if she was talking to me or herself, so I stayed quiet and peered out my window as she continued. "I tried arguing with Bruce and Caroline, but my heart wasn't in it. I don't like their rules for the world, but my own rules betrayed me. Our parents and preachers told us these were the rules we had to live by. I don't know what to do in a situation where there are no rules."

"It's okay, Mom. We have each other, and Aunt Hannah…"

"I'll be praying a lot tonight, asking for guidance," Mom said. "Don't you ever ask God for direction in your life anymore?"

"I can take the good bits from the Bible and hold them close to my heart. I want to do that. But I want to figure out what it means to me and not have everybody else telling me what I should believe. At the end of the season, the farmers around us clear out their fields of all the old cornstalks and debris so they can start new plantings in the spring. New plants need the old spaces cleared of the things that would keep them from growing." I was shocked that I could be so open with Mom.

Mom gave me a "Hmph," then cocked her head toward me and said, "You stole that bit from one of Grandpa's sermons. I recognize it."

"Take the good and use it well," I repeated with a smile on my face.

CHAPTER 10

"Nobody else at this school studies the way we do. Why is that?" I asked during the daily after-school study group.

"Japanese-style studying, I learned it from my parents," Yuki said proudly. "Everything back there is about getting the best score, getting into the best school, and getting the best job. It's the kind of work ethic that brought my parents to the US."

This was met with a chuckle from Dan. "You just studied better than anyone and got the best grades in our school. I sure wasn't going to pass up the opportunity to learn to study like that, and neither was Melanie. And it just sort of grew into a thing we've done ever since."

"Take Chad," Yuki said. "He's so good at basketball, he'll get all kinds of college scholarships to play. His grades are just below ours. You add brains and basketball together, and Chad might play ball for an elite academic school and get a top-tier education for free or close to it. Ask Hannah how expensive the University of Michigan is. Chad's parents could never afford to send him there."

"The stronger our group is, the better all our chances are of getting into good schools and becoming successful adults. Plus, we have a life-long friend base to rely on when we have problems."

I smiled. "I'm glad Angie found you for me."

Angie, Lucy, and Robert were huddled around a table doing science homework with a couple other classmates of mine when I joined them. "Hey, where are the rest of the crew?"

"Kelcee's PMS kicked in, and she's miserable. Joey and I drew straws, and he lost, so he's babysitting her. Hell hath no fury like an angry redhead on the rag."

I giggled at this, but then I realized Robert was laughing, too. "You think our misery is funny, sir?"

"Absolutely not! I have an older sister. I learned quickly to stay out of her way certain times of the month."

We shared a giggle, and I chanced a playful butterfly punch to Robert's bicep. "I'm grouchy for a week, but I won't bite your head off," I said.

"I had my first period when Brian and I were reading comic books in his treehouse," Lucy said thoughtfully. "His parents had to sit him down and have a long talk afterwards. It kind of freaked him out. He got better, though."

Angie grinned. "I don't find the pain an issue. My dad dished out worse. I survived that, I can survive anything." She kept her head, probably because she could feel us all gazing at her in sympathy. It nearly made me cry.

Angie reached over and began playing with my hair absent-mindedly. Robert didn't know what to do, so he did the same thing.

"What are you two weirdoes doing?" I asked, hoping to lighten the mood.

Now it was Robert's turn to flirt. "Looking for fleas," he said boldly.

"Do I look like I have fleas, Robert?"

He smiled. "One can never be sure. Fleas are sneaky."

"Maybe there are fleas in her bra," Angie teased him. "We might have to check."

From across the room came Melanie's voice. "Robert, do you want me to tell your father you're giving women unwanted grooming? If you want to act like a monkey, you can spend Sweetheart Swirl at home eating a banana."

"No, Melanie!"

"Well then, behave yourselves over there!"

"Can I ask a really weird question? Is it normal for kids our age to talk about dating and…you know…" I started.

"Sex?" Robert said the quiet part out loud.

"I expect you learned sex was evil and to only do it with your husband, didn't you?" Melanie asked me. I nodded wordlessly. "Sex is one of the biggest milestones we cross, but you shouldn't be scared of it or think it's evil. I think sex is beautiful, and I'm waiting until I find that special someone to share it with. Of course, everyone here thinks about it. We're waiting to find out if it will happen, who it will happen with, whether we'll like it, or whether we'll regret it. Talking and joking about it makes it less scary. Everyone here feels scared and curious, just like you. I can promise you that."

"We go to the beach together. We've seen each other in swimsuits," Dan said. "We're not dumb. There are some beautiful women in this room. We guys aren't half bad, either. Everybody here thinks about sex. We also know we care about each other and treat each other with respect."

"It's extra real for us," Dee said. "We've been dating for a year. We've had a lot of time to be together, and that makes it hard. I love Chad a lot. Maybe I'm going to want to share everything about me with him, but what happens if we break up? We're not likely to go to the same college."

"It's hard to stop kissing sometimes," Chad admitted. "It feels so right in the moment."

"Because you love each other." Chad's mother suddenly appeared in the room unexpectedly. She wasn't angry. Not one bit. "You respect each other and talk these things through. The fact you and your friends are open and honest about your feelings makes it a lot less likely you'll do something risky. You're good influences on each other."

"Except me," Angie said.

"Don't get me started on you." Chad's mother walked over to Angie and stood over her. "I will never pretend to understand what goes on in your brain. I didn't want my son to have anything to do with you and your friends at first. The thing is, you have never failed to be kind to my son, and you have bravely stood up for him when people have teased him. That gets noticed, Angie Thompson. You love to act bad, but there's a good core in you. One day, you'll figure out how to make that blossom in an incredible way. When it happens, I'm going to say, "I told you so.""

Angie smiled warmly at her. "I won't stop you if you do."

CHAPTER 11

The summons from Mr. Hill was simple: come by his classroom after school. I worried about it all day, wondering what Mr. Hill would say. When I got to his room, Robert was already there.

"I suppose you want to know why I've called you here," he said. He paused and shook his head. "That sounds so cliché, doesn't it?"

"A bit, Dad," Robert said. "You don't have to make it all scary. She'll agree to the terms."

I turned to face him. "You know about this?"

"We talk," he said simply.

"Robert's not the first of my children to attend school here. His sister, Liz, graduated a few years ago. I never want to teach my own children, even though I know my kids would do well. People might think I would give my kids extra attention outside class or be tempted to grade them better than they deserve. If the computer puts them in my class, I make them switch to a different teacher. You aren't my kid. However, I have a sneaking suspicion that my son has a very big crush on you and might be interested in dating you soon. That puts me in a difficult position. I'm going to give you a choice, Sarah. You're scheduled to be in my class again next semester. I can switch you easily enough. Mr. Bellamy is a fine biology teacher, and you'd learn just as much from him as you would from me. If you stay in my class, you cannot date Robert until the school year ends. Going to dances is okay. But no dating each other beyond that."

I thought he was expecting me to argue with him. "We can still hang out as friends, right?"

"Of course, of course!"

"And study together?"

"Absolutely!"

"Then I'll stay in your class, if you'll have me." I looked over at Robert, who gave me a nod of agreement.

"Very well," Mr. Hill said. "That was not the answer I was expecting, but I'll allow it."

"Why?" I asked. "Why did you think I'd choose to leave your class?"

Mr. Hill sat back in his chair. "Because it is what I would have done at your age. I fell in love with someone when I was thirteen. Nothing would have kept me apart from her."

"What happened? You weren't allowed to date?" I asked.

"She's my mom," Robert replied. "They've never fallen out of love."

"What? Really? That's… I've never heard anything like… That's actually kind of beautiful," I was able to realize after a split-second of shock.

"It's true. I don't think I could love Robert's mom any more than I do now."

"Do you think Robert would be like you then?" I asked.

"My wife is cool and calm. He gets his temperament from her. She and I are both incurable romantics, though. We never dated anybody else. We fell in love and hung on to it with all our strength."

I grinned at Robert. "Too soon to say if I'll want to keep you."

"Same here," he said. He smiled at me. I melted a little. I always did.

***

I had a wonderful time at my first dance. I wore a pink, sleeveless dress with spaghetti straps that had a tiny white heart pattern and was tied in the back. It was knee-length, so it wasn't too daring. Robert and Brian wore suits. Lucy had chosen a gorgeous off-shoulder pink dress that had a sporty look to it, matched with white sneakers instead of heels. She was lovely, and Brian did a double-take when he saw her wearing it. Robert and I wore a matching corsage and boutonniere. Brian wore his own boutonniere, but Lucy wanted no part of any flowers because she thought they were mushy. Mom, Brian's parents, and Robert's parents were among the adults chaperoning. Our families all had dinner at Pizza Hut before the dance. Robert and I exchanged Valentine cards before dinner.

We all danced with each other that night, and for the most part, it wasn't a big deal. High school students like to dance in groups, making it easier for you to hang out with all your friends, even if you don't have a date of your own. Within the herd, you could dance with your partner as much as you liked, or dance with your friends if you chose. There was less romantic pressure that way, and hopefully fewer disciplinary problems. Apparently, what you did with your date before or after the dance was supposed to be the romantic part, except for the occasional slow dances for the couples.

At some point during the dance, Angie wound up dancing with Robert and me. Other than the lessons she taught me, I wasn't used to her style. Dancing with Angie was different. She had confidence and a sensuality that no one in our age group had. She flirted with me with her eyes. A touch would happen that was probably innocent, but maybe wasn't. She'd do the same thing to Robert, then she'd mouth the words "watch me" at both of us as she danced. She was teaching us how to seduce each other while seducing us at the same time. When she figured out we understood our lessons, she slipped back into the crowd to find Joey and Kelcee. Half an hour later, a teacher warned us we were getting a little too risqué and needed to tone it down. I looked through the crowd and saw Angie grinning at me. She gave me the thumbs-up sign. Angie's final dance lesson: if the adults are mad at you, you're doing it right.

Robert got the slow dance he dreamed of that night. I made sure of that. When the dance was over, we had to amuse ourselves for a while as our parents finished up their chaperoning duties. Lucy and Brian were playing "basketball" by tossing wads of paper into a trash can from the farthest distance. Lucy won, and she immediately began celebrating.

"Ha-ha! You missed! I get a kiss now! Pay up!" Brian walked over, embraced her, and kissed her warmly. She was stunned.

"W-w-what was that?" she stammered. "You've never kissed me like that! That's weird!" She began blushing.

Brian shrugged and smiled. Robert walked over and put his arms around me. "I wouldn't mind doing that, too."

"We have to wait, remember?" I said, gently chiding him. "But I'll take another dance while we wait."

"There's no music, though."

"Then imagine some for me." We danced silently in our own little world as the janitors began cleaning up the gym around us. I don't know how long we spent doing that, but it ended when I heard a familiar voice in the background.

"Brings back memories of your mother and me in high school," Mr. Hill said warmly. "You two remember what we agreed to, right?"

"We do," Robert said. "I would like to kiss her goodnight, though."

"What makes you think I want to be kissed?" I teased him, ruffling his hair in the process. I absolutely wanted to be kissed! I just didn't think I was allowed to say it so brazenly.

"One kiss on the cheek. That's all I'll allow," Mr. Hill sighed. "In honor of Valentine's Day."

Robert leaned over and kissed me on the cheek. "My first kiss," he said. My mind was racing. I was so excited.

I kissed him on the cheek in return. "Mine, too. I can't wait for summer."

The last act of Valentine's Day was yet to be played out, though I didn't know it at the time. Mom took me home. I went to bed. I was too excited to sleep. I had too much fun and had too much on my mind, so I thought I'd walk over to the other wing to visit the library and find a book to read. I picked out a collection of Abraham Lincoln's speeches, prepared to walk back to my room, but realized Joey, Angie, and Kelcee were in the hallway and were rather drunk. They were making out with each other.

I watched them, mesmerized. They kissed with reckless abandon. Their hands went to places on each other's bodies that I thought should have brought hellfire upon them. No brimstone fell from the heavens, though; only excitement, lust, love, and utter joy were on display. I watched them, spellbound, until one of them managed to open the door to Angie's room, and the three of them rushed inside to continue the show away from my prying eyes. I walked back to my room, forgetting all about Lincoln. I had witnessed something forbidden. I wanted to know what they were feeling. I wanted to understand why they did it. Worst of all, I wanted to understand why I suddenly felt aroused. I shouldn't want this. I can't want this. I ran to my bedroom in a panic. I didn't want to admit to myself why I was running, but deep down, I think I knew.

CHAPTER 12

I learned that night that Mom gets a bit intoxicated from romance, being denied so much of it through a loveless marriage. Once the feeling wore off, she was a bit more circumspect. She still adored Robert, but she readily admitted she had no idea how it could ever work out because he wasn't a Christian and wouldn't be accepted by the family.

"Since when does the family get any say in my life?" I growled back. "They didn't do much to help us all these years." I didn't think I should argue with her, or I might not be allowed to date him at all. I wasn't happy, and I made sure she knew it.

She didn't seem surprised. "I understand how you feel. I think you have every right to that opinion. I don't feel like arguing about this today. Maybe I never will. I'm just letting you know I **should** argue this point as your mother and as a Christian."

***

Angie wandered into my room one night and flopped down on the bed. I was doing my homework at my desk, and she seemed content watching me for a while before announcing the reason she was visiting. "Your mom's having a fit. I think she's scared of you and Robert. Hannah is trying to talk to her."

I sighed. "Not this again. I can't date him yet. We're not dating. We're just really, really good friends."

"Bullshit!" Angie laughed.

I smiled. "That's what I'm supposed to say. Yeah, I like him. I like him a lot."

"I noticed. I see the way you two look at each other. Have you had the birds and the bees talk yet?"

"When I was twelve. Mom gave it to me."

"If things between you two get serious and you want to know more, let me know. I can already tell your mom won't be a lot of help in that regard. I suspect when she did have sex, she didn't enjoy it much. She wouldn't know how to tell you how to do it, so you and your partner would be happy."

"I saw you three making out the other night," I said.

"Were you spying, you little perv?" Angie admonished playfully.

"No, I couldn't sleep and went to get a book from the library. When I went to leave, you three were there."

"So, what did you think?" Angie leaned in, biting her lower lip.

"I thought it was hot!"

Angie raised an eyebrow. "Did you, now?" She smiled. "Even when I kissed Kelcee?"

"I shouldn't have thought that," I said softly. "But I did." I paused for a moment. There was a question forming in my brain, and Angie saw it.

"You're thinking about something. You can always ask me, you know. I'll tell you the truth, always."

"Does it feel good?"

"Does what feel good, making out?" Angie asked playfully.

"Yeah, and…sex," I said quietly.

"Uh, duh. Yes," she said. "I love it. There are lots of different things we do together and different things we try. Some I like more than others. The ones I don't like, I don't do. Kelcee and Joey enjoy different things, and we all make sure we make each other happy."

And then it spilled out of my mouth. "I want to experience that someday. I don't want to be like Mom, and I don't know if I want to wait as long as she did either. I want to find someone who cares about me and who I love, and I want to have what you have."

"No, you want to have a love that will last you the rest of your life. What I have isn't permanent. Joey and Kelcee have college ahead of them. When they leave, I start over. Maybe you'll have to deal with that when you and Robert graduate, too."

I got up from my desk and crawled onto the bed next to her. "How do I even start thinking about dating Robert when I have to worry about saying goodbye?"

"Because you love him more than anything else in the world," Angie said. "Sometimes you get lucky, and goodbye isn't forever. We're not going to let Joey forget about us just because he's going away to school. He's got two hot high school girls who love fucking him back home. If he's smart, he'll remember that."

"What do I even do with you?" I sighed. "You're like a big sister who wants to tempt me to the dark side."

"I can be many things to you, Sarah, but I will never be your sister." Angie smiled and hugged me. "It would make some things really awkward if they happen, and I don't want that."

"Like what?" I asked innocently.

Angie sighed and rolled her eyes. "G'night, kid." And with that, she got up and left.

CHAPTER 13

Dad received his notification of the divorce proceedings while in jail. Chandra laid out what we were going to ask for. Mom wanted her personal effects and her Powell name. Because Dad was in jail and Mom didn't have a job, nobody was making payments on the house. It would make sense for the house to be sold. After all debts from the marriage were paid, Mom would get most of the remaining money in exchange for giving up spousal support. Mom wanted full custody without any visitation rights offered to Dad. From what I heard, Dad's response was an angry phone call to Chandra's office, calling her a whore and a meddler. He was not negotiating and not signing anything. Given that answer, Chandra went ahead with the process without him. If we had to, we'd get a default judgment and get everything we asked for. In the end, Grandpa Brenner's lawyer contacted Chandra and asked if he could buy out Mom's share of the house. To be blunt, Grandpa and Grandma didn't want Dad living with them. Mom didn't care where the money came from, and so she had Chandra make the deal.

Just as Hannah found herself willing to take Erin on for her managerial skills, she found Mom too good a cook to lose. She asked her if she wanted to work full-time as a chef and household assistant, taking a load off Erin's plate. Mom jumped at the chance and readily agreed. Erin would transition into becoming a full-time agent and publicist, and Mom would become the house manager once she was fully trained. Besides cooking and shopping, she'd oversee the contract workers who handled maid service, gardening, and maintenance. There would be no more dependence on other people's charity or my father's capricious whims. She would earn her own money for the first time since she was married.

***

I found my mother dusting the shelves and singing hymns in a cheery voice one evening. Strictly speaking, there wasn't an urgent need for her to do this. Hannah had a maid who came by a couple times a week to clean the house. Mom didn't mind addressing emergencies that popped up in between visits, but this was weird. She appeared relaxed and radiant in a way I'd never observed before. I complimented her when I saw her and asked what happened. She suddenly blushed.

"Erin and Hannah have been teaching me some relaxation techniques," she said nervously. "I've been way too tensed up lately. I need to focus on things if I'm going to handle my new responsibilities."

On the surface, that sounded logical and good. The only problem was that she didn't seem as relaxed as she did giddy. I didn't know what to make of it all.

Erin was in the main wing of the house when I found her, and I asked her what was wrong with my mother. She smiled enigmatically. "Nothing's wrong. Quite the opposite—things are better than they've been in a long time."

"What did you teach her?"

"Ask your mother if you're curious," she said.

"She said it was relaxation techniques," I replied.

Erin shook her head. "I suppose I shouldn't be surprised. This might be a milk and cookies sort of thing." She took me into the kitchen and sat me down at the table. Milk and cookies soon followed, and she sat down beside me. Angie walked into the kitchen as well and quickly started eating cookies along with me.

"Your mom has major orgasm face," Angie said. "Did she learn how to masturbate or something?"

Milk came flying out of my nose as I started laughing at exactly the wrong time.

"I was about to explain these matters to Sarah in a very professional and adult way…and you go and say that!" Erin was laughing. She got up to find a dish towel to clean up my mess.

"That's dirty! It's wrong to play with yourself! That's what I was always taught."

"It's fun!" Angie said. "I love it."

"It is a very normal thing that most people do now and then," Erin said. "Your old church doesn't like it because it allows you as a human being to enjoy pleasure and sexuality. They want you to think sex is dirty or only for procreation. Your father never gave Tina any enjoyment from the sex they had. She was just a vessel for him to impregnate, whether she wanted the experience or not."

"Did you do anything to her?" I asked.

Erin shook her head at the ceiling. "I gave her a book and a pep talk. She didn't understand why not being with a man didn't bother me. I told her there were ways to make myself happy that didn't involve a penis. She'd never experienced them because she'd been taught the same things you were."

"Do you know how?" Angie asked. "I can teach you if you want."

"You will do no such thing!" Erin chuckled, swatting at her with the dish towel. "Tina is getting used to living in a house with three bisexual women. She's still struggling with the concept. If you need to play, you have Kelcee to play with. Let Tina be the mother here. At least give her the first chance. We can always do it if she won't."

Mom came into the kitchen to start preparing dinner for the evening. She acted a bit more normal. She also peered rather nervously at the three of us looking at her with silly grins. "Did I miss something?"

"You did, Tina. You did. When you're done with that book you don't have and aren't reading, give it to your daughter. She needs it, too," Erin said.

For a split second, I thought Mom was going to lose her temper. She caught herself at the last moment. "I'll discuss that with her in private," she replied, a hint of frosty displeasure in her voice.

"As is your right," Erin said. "But remember all the years you lost because other people didn't value your rights as a woman. Don't force your daughter to tread the same path any more than she already has."

Mom nodded. "I think I'd like to be able to harness the feelings I am feeling before I teach my daughter how to do so."

"That's a fair statement. I can accept that. Are we doing lasagna or spaghetti tonight, Tina? I can't remember what we decided."

With that, the tempest passed. Mom and Erin got down to work on preparing the meal as if nothing had happened.

***

Since the dance, Brian and Lucy came to realize things had changed between them. Melanie, who was always quick to spot trouble in the group, dragged them aside and had a long talk with them about their friendship and what they wanted to happen in the future. It was to no one's surprise that they announced they were now a couple, although they were still very much learning what that meant.

Lucy decided she wanted to invite me over to sleep at her place. I took her up on it on a Friday night. To no one's surprise, she walked across the street and dragged Brian over to hang out with us. We played board games, baked cookies, and drank hot chocolate. Lucy's mom sent us to bed around eleven and sent Brian home. We weren't sleepy at first and talked quietly in her bed for a while. At first, it wasn't anything memorable. I was even getting sleepy listening to her.

"Why are boys weird?" she asked me, snapping me back to attention.

"Because we are awesome and they have trouble coping with that," I chuckled. "They probably think we're weird, too. Boobs might also have something to do with it. Puberty gives us all kinds of weird hormones and PMS. Guys have their own things to deal with. They're changing, too."

Lucy laughed. "He's started shaving."

"So have we. Just different places."

She started snickering and fell back on the bed laughing. "True!" She paused and stared thoughtfully at the ceiling. "Brian and I have been play-fighting and rolling around and doing stupid shit together for years. I've kissed him before, and the only thing he did was make faces and spit at me! Now he kisses me, and my heart goes crazy."

"I don't even have to kiss Robert for that to happen."

"You two are too cute together," she giggled. "We're going to have a great summer."

"Don't take this the wrong way, but have you ever kissed a girl before?' I asked.

"Maybe," she said slyly. "Why do you want to know?'

"I saw Angie, Kelcee, and Joey making out. She and Kelcee…that was something!"

Lucy giggled. "I don't doubt that! I've never seen them going at it. Melanie walked in on them having sex together a couple of times when we were in junior high. She told us the details. Freaky! Some of us tried kissing each other to see if we could figure out what the big deal was. Didn't really do anything for us. If you're curious, we can kiss," Lucy chuckled. "Then you won't have to worry about it anymore."

She leaned over and motioned for me to kiss her. I'd only kissed Robert on the cheek. I'd never given anyone a real kiss. I'd only known what I'd seen Angie do, and I knew that wasn't how a first kiss should work. I leaned over and softly kissed her lips to start, followed by a second, slightly more energetic kiss. She giggled at me.

"Not bad for a first try. What did you think?"

"It was nice. I liked it. I'm not in love with you, so I didn't feel fireworks or anything like that."

"I should hope not! One boyfriend is plenty for me. I have enough drama. Don't kiss me goodnight, though. I think you might get addicted to it."

I fell asleep next to her, and we woke up in each other's arms. We were somewhat embarrassed and didn't say anything more about it.

CHAPTER 14

Second-semester biology was going to tackle the topic of evolution. This didn't bother me a great deal. If it was explained to me well enough, I could pass a test on it. I just didn't know if it was going to change my mind. Mom was more vocal in her displeasure that I was learning anything about it at all, but she genuinely liked Mr. Hill and wanted to steer a middle course to keep the peace.

The Bible says we are fearfully and wonderfully made. We are awe-inspiring creations. The level of complexity our bodies have is truly amazing, and it all comes from one sperm and one egg, along with the genetic instructions contained within them. Listening to Mr. Hill talk about evolution, I began to realize just how incredible all life is and how interrelated we all are. I began to have doubts about what I had been taught. I didn't want to talk to Mom about them. I wanted to learn more about the subject, and I went looking in the mansion library to see if Hannah kept any books on evolution on the shelves. She did. One of them was an old college textbook she had used during her school days. The margins were full of notes. Hannah had poured out her thoughts and frustrations into her textbook, and reading what she wrote was like tapping into her consciousness.

We were taught Scripture was inerrant. The transgressions of Adam and Eve in the Garden of Eden brought a sinful nature upon every human ever born. Jesus had to come to Earth to die on the cross to make a way for humankind to receive pardon and have a chance at Heaven. If there were no Garden of Eden, no talking snake, no Adam—there would be no reason for any sacrifice to be made. The Bible would not be inerrant. It would not be the word of God. It would just be human words. The imaginations of scribes and storytellers seeking to understand the universe in ancient times. Hannah understood that. Hannah had been where I was now. I grabbed the book and ran to find her. She was in bed reading in her room.

"What brings you to see me so late?" she asked with a curious, but kind expression on her face.

I showed her the book. "I was reading your notes."

She smiled. "Is this an angry visit?"

"No," I said softly. "I think we understand each other."

"The veil is lifting?" she asked.

I nodded. "Things make more sense now."

She reached over and hugged me tightly. "You need to talk to your mother, though."

"She won't be happy."

"She won't be. I think she'll listen to you, though. Unlike my family."

When I went back to our living quarters, Mom had already retired to bed. I didn't want to wake her up, and so I only softly tapped on the door, hoping she wouldn't hear.

"Come in," she said. So much for my luck. She was at her desk writing. "What are you still doing up on a school night for?"

"Talking with Hannah," I said.

"About what?"

I showed Mom the textbook, and she read through the same things I did. Her brow furrowed as she kept reading.

"I guess I know why Hannah is the way she is," I said, feeling the need to say something. I sat down on her bed and waited for her to make her judgment.

Mom closed the textbook and handed it to me. "You were having questions about what you learned? Is that why you went to the library?"

"Yes," I said firmly. "I want to know more about what I'm learning."

"When you have finished with this, I want to read it myself." I wasn't expecting her to say that. "How are you feeling now?"

"Scared," I said. "Aunt Hannah said I should talk to you about this, but I'm scared you'll make us leave this place, and I'm only just starting to be happy for the first time in my life."

"All those times your teachers said your faith wasn't firm— they knew something I didn't want to see. Your father said Hannah was always like that, too. Always the rebel. Always questioning things. Always the better person, in the end." She got up from her desk and sat down beside me. "We are not leaving here. You can put that silly idea out of your head immediately."

I hugged her. "Thank you, Mom!"

"I will not be telling Grandpa and Grandma Brenner about this. I want to talk to Jerry about a few things. If my daughter is taking an interest in science, I need to be prepared to support those ambitions. I need to have a chat with Hannah as well."

"You're not angry with me?"

Mom gave me a soft cuff on the butt. "There's your spanking, insolent child. I am not your father. I may be disappointed in you not having the faith I think you should have, but I love you for being the person you are. I'm not comfortable with what I believe now after following Hannah's logic. I need to understand science better. I wonder if we were all lied to."

The next day, I told Mr. Hill that my mom was going to be looking for him, and he appeared worried at first until I explained everything that had happened. "I'll call her tonight," he said. "She's not behaving like most creationist parents I've dealt with in my career. Open-mindedness is the last thing I expect from them. I'm glad you're studying on your own. Don't just take what I tell you to be true. Check as many sources as you want. That's how scientists do it in the real world." He smiled at me. "Give me an example of something neat you've learned this week."

I paused and smiled. "The idea that species have the same basic toolkit that directs how our bodies form on a genetic level and how those genes prove the evolutionary path we've traveled. Everything makes sense in a way it didn't before."

Robert walked into his dad's classroom and gave me a nudge. "We need to get going. I don't want to walk all the way to Yuki's house!"

"Sorry! My mom wants to talk to your dad. I was just letting him know."

"Sarah says she likes science," Mr. Hill said with an impish smile. "That's bonus points for getting permission this summer." Robert grinned at me, and the two of us hurried off.

Mom and Mr. Hill did have that conversation. Mr. Hill wouldn't say anything to me about what was said, though Robert noted his father deeply respected her. All Mom would say was that she believed God created the world, but how He had done so was His business, and she'd be content with whatever method brought me to her.

CHAPTER 15

Robert and I got to know each other a little more with every week that passed. I liked what I saw in him. His parents adored me, and Mom thought he was a fine young man who knew how to treat women properly. By March, we were spending time at each other's houses with our parents' permission. He enjoyed a wide variety of music. We fell into the habit of sitting in his room for an hour listening to music until my mom came to pick me up. He introduced me to the Beatles, the Rolling Stones, Prince, Steely Dan, Michael Jackson, and the Doobie Brothers. Since I lived in the country and was a little further away from the light pollution in town, Robert began bringing his telescope out to our house to look at the stars with me. His parents would sit in the house and talk with my mother, Erin, and Hannah while they waited for us. From what I heard, their conversations were quite lively and enjoyable.

On one of those nights, we were outside gazing at the moon through his telescope when he asked me a question I hadn't expected. "Is it hard for you living here?"

"Not compared to where I used to live," I said. "It is different. Sometimes it is weird. But I like it here. I want to stay."

"Has your mother changed her mind about you dating someone who isn't a Christian?"

"She thinks the world of you. None of that matters now."

"She's changed a lot. Dad says he's amazed by how she's opening her mind to new ideas. I'm glad."

"Still planning on asking me out?" I said, giving him a playful hug.

"Maybe," he grinned.

"I thought Sherri Morehouse had a crush on you."

"Sherri likes country music and can't stand rock. She hates science, too. My sister and I were both into science from the time we could walk. We loved it so much that we had a hard time making friends because kids thought we were weird. My sister is still a loner by nature, and I learned how to be one from watching her. Melanie and her group pulled me into their world because I loved science, and they did, too. It took a while to get used to their personalities and develop my own, but I did. That's why I'm so excited to see you doing that, too."

"There's so much I don't know about the world. I like having you all show me new things. The things you like are interesting. I love your passion. I have things I'm passionate about, and you're interested in them, too. We make a good team." I hugged him very tightly and kissed him on the lips. I let myself stay close to him and feel his body heat. "My answer is 'yes,' by the way. I want you to ask me out." I quickly let him go in case any eyes from inside the house might be watching.

He smiled and then quickly turned back to gaze into his telescope. He stood there shivering.

"Are you okay?"

"Yeah," he said. "I just can't move right now."

"Did your eyeball freeze to the lens or something?"

His answer came in a soft, deeply embarrassed voice. "Erection," he mumbled.

I knew what those were. Mom had explained that in her sex talk when I was younger.

"I'm sorry," he said quietly.

"Don't be."

"Huh?"

"I've got a guy who thinks I'm beautiful and can't hide it." We both chuckled; my attempt at a joke helped lighten the mood. "Let me see the moon while you take a deep breath and try to relax." I nudged him out of the way and started looking at lunar craters. "Tell me when it's safe."

About a minute later, he quietly gave the all-clear announcement. We didn't talk about anything other than astronomy for the rest of the night. We didn't have to. Nobody inside the house noticed what had happened outside, but it was obvious when we came in that *something* had happened.

"You two are acting funny," Mr. Hill said. "Did we miss something outside?"

"We were making plans for the summer," I said, smiling at him.

Being a high school teacher gave Mr. Hill a lot of experience decoding adolescent facial expressions. The way we looked at each other told him all he needed to know. "I see," he said and smiled. "Summer, though. Not spring."

"She knows," Robert said.

***

I gave Mom Hannah's textbook when we finished our study of evolution in class. In return, she gave me the book Erin had given her. There were two bookmarks inside. "There's the section on self-pleasure," she said. "You'll enjoy it." She paused. "I bookmarked the chapter on bisexuality, too. It helped explain what goes on around this house." She said it in an odd voice. There wasn't a hint of condemnation in her tone, but I couldn't place what she was feeling.

I picked the second selection first. It was a very thorough explanation of why people are gay, lesbian, and bisexual, explained through science and not superstition. Angie wasn't weird or evil. She was just a little bit different, and that was okay. I aimlessly flipped through the pages for a moment and was stunned to see the book included drawings of sexual positions. Mom had only explained one to me, but there were so many ways people could have sex. I was spellbound. I learned how Angie and Kelcee did it when they were together. I finally reached the first tab my mother left, and I discovered how to make myself happy. I stayed up far too late that night. I came down to breakfast the next morning looking glassy-eyed. Mom gave me a lecture about doing too much research and too little sleeping…and a very large mug of coffee to drink on the way to school. Angie just giggled at me.

***

After dinner that night, Angie invited me up to her room. "I know what you did last night. What did you think?"

"It's kind of overwhelming. You do all that…"

She smiled. "Not all at once! You don't open a cookbook and make every recipe you read. You just know there are different ones you can try, and you try the ones you like when you're in the mood."

I let out a deep sigh of relief. "It is all still very intense. I'm having trouble wrapping my head around it. The things I can do. The things people can do to me."

"Sometimes it is best not to overthink life. Do simple things first and get good at those. You might find that's what makes you the happiest, and that's okay. The simple things are amazing on their own."

"I'm not ready for that yet," I said. "But I am curious now. Robert gets excited thinking about me. Now I can get excited thinking about him."

"He told you that?" Angie asked with surprise.

"I hugged him while he was looking through the telescope. He couldn't move for a bit."

Angie fell on her bed laughing. "You are a tease, Sarah!"

"I didn't mean to!" I lay down beside her.

"I believe it. But you know how to get to him now, and you can do it whenever you like if you're smart. You'll have him eating out of your hand." She smiled at me. "I think you're going to enjoy sex when your time comes. You'll be a fun partner."

"You think?"

"I do. I'll be jealous of Robert. You're beautiful. If he doesn't take you, I'm going to ask you out someday."

I blushed. "What are Kelcee and Joey going to say about that?"

"Wanna double date?"

I whacked her with a pillow, and the fight was on. We wound up getting yelled at by Hannah for disturbing her work, and I was banished to my side of the house for the rest of the evening.

CHAPTER 16

Teachers can be a gossipy bunch. Since Mom was active in the PTA, she turned up at school regularly to do volunteer work, and the staff genuinely appreciated her willingness to support a school I had only just joined. The news gradually got out that Jerry Hill's son was in love with me and that our two families were getting ready to grant us permission to date when the school year ended. Mr. Hill took some good-natured ribbing from his fellow teachers, many of whom were parents themselves. He embraced the situation in his own unique way. On the bulletin board in his classroom, a counter appeared one day proudly announcing the number of days until school was out, and Mr. Hill would update it every morning. I got teased about that, too, and I didn't care at all.

***

Our friends try to support each other whenever we can. Whenever the athletes among us are playing, we try to be there to cheer them on. I loved watching Dee play volleyball and talked Mom into going with me. We met Melanie and Dan there, and we all went to get a seat when Melanie noticed Miss Reimer in the bleachers.

Miss Reimer was my English teacher for the semester. At twenty-six, she was the youngest teacher in the building. She didn't seem like a high school teacher—more like a college student you'd find at a bar in Ann Arbor. She knew English literature inside and out and made no secret of the fact that we were there to learn, not screw around, in her class from the moment we walked in. I found her a great teacher, but I was intimidated by her.

"What's she doing here? That's the last person I want to run into when I'm out!" Melanie said.

Mom saw her and waved. To our astonishment, she stood up and waved back and motioned us to join her. The three of us exchanged looks of dread, but Mom was already walking up the stairs.

"I hope there's extra credit for us in this," Dan sighed. We followed along behind.

"What brings you out tonight?" she asked us. "You all have homework to do, remember?"

"Our friend Dee is playing," Melanie said. "We're here for her."

Dee was warming up on the court at the time and let loose a vicious spike of the ball. "That's her," I said. "She's the Beast."

"That brings back memories," Miss Reimer said. "I used to play varsity volleyball for South Lyon when I was in high school. Been meaning to catch a game for the longest time, and my schedule finally worked out. Brings back a lot of good memories."

"I'm almost finished with that volume of Tennyson you loaned me," Mom said.

"No rush, Tina. I'm glad I have someone to share it with."

"You two are friends?" Melanie asked.

Mom sighed. "I used to be an English Literature major in college once upon a time. I didn't realize how much I missed it until I got away from Daniel. I asked your principal if anyone on staff had expertise in the matter and could recommend some books to help me get back into reading. She introduced me to Miss Reimer."

"Once summer gets here and I have actual time to breathe, we're going to get together and nerd out. I miss having friends I can read poetry with and not feel weird."

"Why should you feel weird?" Dan asked. "Poetry can be beautiful. I might want to write one someday when I get brave enough to tell someone I love them."

"Did you have someone in mind?" I teased him.

"Maybe," he said. Melanie was watching the warmups on the court. He was looking at her the same way Robert did at me. I saw it. Mom and Miss Reimer saw it, too.

"That would be a beautiful thing to do, Dan," Mom said. "Ask Miss Reimer to read through it if you think that will make your chances better."

"Hey, now! I'm supposed to be the scary, mean teacher here! Don't make me likable!" She was trying not to smile as she spoke, and she was failing miserably at it.

"You're off the clock. You can let them see who you truly are," Mom said.

Robert and Yuki showed up late and joined us in the stands. We had a wonderful time cheering Dee on, and Miss Reimer totally outed herself as a volleyball player by the enthusiasm she showed and the advice she yelled to the team on the floor. Mom also slipped up and called Miss Reimer "Charli" once, and we had to promise to keep that a secret, or she'd chain us up in the detention hall until we graduated.

On the way home, I told Mom I never imagined Miss Reimer could be normal. She laughed when I said this.

"She's not so different from all of you," Mom said. "In fact, once you stop being her students, you might find she slides into the role of being an older friend. I certainly want to get to know her better. I love being able to share my interests with friends. It's why being around Erin and Hannah is so important to me."

We gradually fell into a rhythm where Robert and I would have dinner at each other's houses once a week. It was our turn to host, and he rode home from our study session at Chad's house with Mom. We had thought Angie would not be joining us for dinner. We were wrong. Angie's plans for the evening had fallen through, and she sat down to join us.

"I had your dad as a teacher when I was in ninth grade," she said.

"I know," Robert said. "I heard about the time in his class you were wearing a skirt, and you sat back too far in your chair and fell over. No panties…"

Erin's jaw dropped. "You did what? I never heard about this!"

Angie laughed. "I remember that! Joey dared me. Your dad gave me detention for a week! That's the time I told you I was helping with the school play."

Erin shook her head. "Fortunately, the statute of limitations ran out on that crime."

Mom focused on her salad and pretended she was on some other planet. Hannah was admiring the cracks in the ceiling. I was laughing my ass off, and Robert sat there looking at Angie like she was some kind of madwoman.

We managed to finish our meal without any more weirdness. Afterward, Robert and I went off to my room to listen to music. Angie heard us singing and popped her head in my room. We spent the entire evening with the stereo going, singing together. Not perfectly—we weren't in the same league with the greats of rock and roll—but we had the time of our lives. I loved being with Robert, but having Angie together with us added some extra spice to the mix.

"I hear you like Sarah," Angie said.

"She's really special," Robert agreed. "I can't date her until summer. But I am looking forward to it."

"Don't make her cry, okay? She's had a shitty life up until she came here. I want her to be happy."

"Me too," he said. "Maybe that's something we should work on together. Hanging out with you is fun. We should do it more often."

Angie's jaw dropped slightly. Her composure cracked for a moment before it was replaced with a devilish smile. "You are dangerous, Robert Hill. Just remember I am, too. I might decide to take both of you."

"Hush, demon! You already have Joey and Kelcee!" I laughed. "Go play with them if you're bored."

"I plan on it," she said seductively. With that, she blew us a kiss and left us to say our goodbyes.

I had a very vivid dream that night of Robert and me making out, only for Angie to interrupt us. Instead of the moment ending, Angie was pulled into bed with us, and the three of us had sex. I woke up with a start and instinctively prayed for forgiveness for ever thinking such a thing. But the thoughts didn't go away after I prayed. The thoughts excited and terrified me in equal measure.

CHAPTER 17

We had an assignment to do figure drawing for art class. Lucy suggested we both get Brian to model for us. We went and asked him after school, and he said he might do it if it wasn't too weird.

"How is modeling for us weird?" I asked. "Pick a pose, get comfortable, and let us draw you. It might take a couple hours, but you'll have our undying gratitude."

"Do I have to pose nude?" he asked with a smile.

"This is high school, you pervert!" Lucy laughed. "Nobody's posing nude."

"I'm thinking chaise lounge…a cute blonde feeding me grapes…" Brian was having way too much fun with this.

"Nobody wants to feed you grapes, either. I don't want to feed you grapes, and I'm your girlfriend!" Lucy sniped at him playfully.

"That would be a funny picture. I wonder if we could get Robert to pose with him and feed him grapes?" I said with a smile.

"That's not funny. That's weird!" Lucy said.

"I like that idea. Have Robert feed me grapes while holding a sign that says, 'They made me do this!' Mr. Chatsworth would get a laugh out of that."

I told Robert what Brian had in mind. Robert instantly liked the idea and agreed. We made up a sign, bought a bag of grapes from the grocery store, and borrowed one of Aunt Hannah's silver trays. We also borrowed a couple of togas and some period sandals from the school's drama club. Everyone came over to my house, and we had the modeling session in our living room. It was only then that we discovered nobody could keep their composure, stay still, or draw coherently. We gave up, and each sketched our own boyfriends in their togas. We received A grades on our drawings, and Mr. Chatsworth was none the wiser for what might have been.

Bless his heart, Robert came by my locker and asked when he was getting paid. He was kidding, of course. He did it for friendship and nothing else. I looked to see if there were any security guards or teachers around to see us. With the coast clear, I kissed him in front of my locker. Not on the cheek, either. Right on the lips. That was totally against the deal I made with Mr. Hill. I didn't care. God help me, I'm just like Angie now. She totally would have done that.

***

It was a couple of weeks before spring break. I was sound asleep in bed when I felt a nudge. It was Angie.

"What time is it anyway?" I mumbled.

"1:30 maybe?"

"Why are you here? Haven't you got anything wicked you could be doing right now?"

"I wore Joey and Kelcee out tonight, so no."

I could have lived without knowing that. My senses were starting to kick in. I could smell Angie's shampoo and body wash. She was wearing her bathrobe.

"They want to talk to you."

I sat up in bed. "What? Do you know how much trouble I'll get in talking to them if Mom catches me?"

"Don't get caught then. Are you coming or not?"

"This had better be good." I got out of bed, grabbed my bathrobe from its hook on my door, threw it on over my satin pajamas, and quietly trekked behind Angie through the hallway and into the main wing of the house. She opened her bedroom door and walked in. I followed behind. Kelcee and Joey were in bed under the covers, snuggling. Judging by the empty beer bottles and the scent of marijuana in the air, there had been mischief aplenty going on earlier.

"What do you want?" I asked them.

"Angie is talking about you way too much these days," Kelcee said. "You've really been a good friend to Melanie, and I appreciate that. I wanted you to know we like you as a friend. Angie chose you well."

"She's pretty," Joey said. "I like her long hair."

"You said you liked mine short!" Angie sputtered, glaring at him with a look of utter annoyance.

"I like your hair short," Kelcee said in response. "He's always liked it long."

"Why didn't you ever say anything?"

"What makes you happy makes me happy."

"Ugh! I'm growing it out again. Sarah likes it when I play with her hair. She should have some to play with, too."

"I need a favor from you, Sarah." Joey's voice was calm and reassuring.

"What is it?"

"Take care of Angie and Kelcee for me. I'm going to miss them when I leave in the fall."

I was taken aback by this and smiled a bit, despite myself. "That's what Kelcee's here to do. She's Angie's girlfriend."

"Angie's a handful. Kelcee might need help from time to time. You and Robert are closer to Angie than anyone else in our group."

I smiled at Angie. "She's been so kind and understanding since I moved in. I adore her. Even if she's a bit of a bad influence on me."

"The best kind of bad influence." Angie tossed her bathrobe on her desk. She was wearing an oversized T-shirt underneath. She gave me a hug that lasted just a bit too long to be simply friendly.

"I do plan on coming back to South Lyon when I can," Joey said. "My family is here. Kelcee says she's going to try to come to Michigan Tech when she graduates. There aren't any guarantees, though. We all know it. If I meet someone incredible there, I'm going to follow my heart. High school relationships don't normally last forever."

"Robert's parents' did," I protested.

"They were lucky," Kelcee said. "I'm hoping I'll be lucky, too. But I wouldn't bet on it. I plan to enjoy every moment we have together and whatever happens after that, happens."

"They don't have to wait for me," Joey said. "If they find the love of their life while I'm gone, they know I am going to cheer them on. I just thought you should know."

Kelcee cuddled up next to Joey. She wasn't willing to let go yet. Angie was different. Angie could break things off if she wanted. I understood why I was here. Angie and I were being given permission to hook up. That's not at all what I wanted. Was it?

"So, you'll be cheering Robert and me on?" I asked, trying to steer the discussion back on course.

"Absolutely. Robert is an amazing guy," Joey said. "Watching him fall in love has been fun."

"We're agreed then. I'm going to date Robert. That's my priority and focus."

"We wouldn't have it any other way," Joey replied. "If things don't work out with the two of you, however, you might have other options if you were brave enough to consider them. Just saying."

"And what would those be?" I asked him.

"Depends on how the future goes, doesn't it?" Angie chuckled. "I would date you in a heartbeat. If I'm in bed with you and these two show up, you could broaden your horizons in a hurry."

What terrified me in that moment was the mental picture she was drawing for me and the fact I wasn't rejecting it outright. It would never happen, not in a million years. But if it did…

Kelcee looked at me carefully. "You fascinate me. You act like you're above all this, and you're such a good girl. You aren't, though. You were good because you had to be. You didn't have a choice. Now that you're free, you are going to be every bit as perverted as we are, and you will embrace it with every fiber of your being. You don't believe me. That's fine. I never thought I'd be anything other than a good girl, either. When we're all adults, you'll be the one in the threesome, not me. I'll grow up and settle down. You, Robert, and Angie will play house until you die of old age because you're naïve enough to think you could actually make it work."

Kelcee was blunt, but she always told you what she was thinking. Angie just smiled stupidly at me. I was tired and annoyed by all this, even if Kelcee knew me better than I wanted to admit. I was pissed off, and I wasn't going to let this provocation go unanswered. I didn't care who heard me.

"You guys are pathetic. You're cowards. You have been playing for three years, and you haven't learned the first thing about what love means!"

"Who are you to lecture us?" Kelcee shot back.

"Shut the fuck up! You have lived such easy lives. This is all a game for you. Oh, look at us! We're polyamorous! We're edgy! We're dangerous! You're fucking lazy! Kelcee, you are an amazing woman. Angie, you're so special to me that I am questioning my own sexuality. Joey, you could have these two for the rest of your life, and you haven't got the balls to commit to them. They've done everything for you. I don't dare ask what they've done to you. And you're just going to go off to college and think you'll get a better deal? Fuck that and fuck you if you believe that!" I said, out of breath.

"Life happens," Joey replied. "We don't always get what we want."

"Damn right. My dad hated me from the moment I was born. My dad was mean and abusive to me and my mom my whole life, and my family and my church let it happen. God didn't come down and save me. God couldn't be bothered. I don't even know if I believe in God any longer! Everything I thought I believed about the world got torched, and I'm watching it burn. I shouldn't have anything to cling to, but I do, because I'm a fucking idiot. I believe in love. Mom loves me. Hannah loves me. I'm going to believe someone special is out there waiting for me, and I'll fight to make that person happy. I will be damned if I let anything stand in my way of making that dream happen, and I certainly won't give up on it because of little things that could be overcome if only you bothered to try!" With that, I stalked out of the room and slammed the door.

I suddenly found myself face-to-face with Erin and Hannah, whom I had woken up with my tirade. "Sorry," I said. "I'm not in the mood for idiots tonight."

Erin had the hint of a smile on her sleepy face. "They need to be yelled at now and then. I'd suggest getting out of here before your mother finds you on this side of the house."

I walked back to my room in the dark. I noticed a light on in my mother's room and knocked softly at the door.

"What are you doing up at this hour?" she asked when she opened the door.

"I was going to ask you the same question," I replied, deliberately not answering her.

"A lot on my mind," she said.

"Want to talk about it?" I asked. She nodded and let me in. We sat down on her bed together.

"I asked Charli if she wanted to do lunch over spring break," Mom said. She's open to it.

"Good!" I said happily. "So, what's the problem?"

"I asked Erin once if she'd ever date a man again. She said no. She has male friends, but she finds the only peace she really can get now is with Hannah. I had a terrible nightmare about your father tonight. I woke up and prayed about it. That's what I'm supposed to do." Mom paused and looked at me. "I didn't feel any peace. Nothing but darkness. And then I thought of Charli comforting me, and I freaked out."

I hugged her. "Don't jump to conclusions. You were under a lot of stress. Given the fact that the two of you are getting to be good friends, having someone like Charli by your side when you're really hurting is natural. It's your brain telling you to find someone and talk—like you're doing now with me."

"That's a relief," Mom sighed.

"Brains are weird, though. All kinds of things pop up in dreams." I smiled and hugged her. "I still have nightmares about him, too. I suppose we always will."

"This feels weird to me, giving you advice."

She smiled at me. "It does. Don't get used to it, dear. I'll be back on top of my game in the morning."

"You'd better be. I'm fourteen, going on fifteen. I'm not about to make it easy on you."

"I'll remember you said that, dear. Now get to sleep."

Kelcee and Joey stayed for breakfast the next morning. I expected they wouldn't talk to me at all. To my great surprise, they both hugged me when I came into the dining room.

"We had a long talk after you left," Joey said. "I think we're agreed we need to at least try to make this work even though I'm away." Kelcee seemed relieved. Angie's expression was harder to read.

"I apologize for being rough with you," I said. "It was late, and I was cranky."

Mom looked at me intently. "Were you making the rounds last night? Who else did you give advice to?"

"We wanted to talk to her," Kelcee said with a sly smile on her face. "We all need to be put in our place from time to time. Sarah certainly does. Angie filled me in on where to tickle you if I want you in submission in a hurry. I'll be more than willing to use that knowledge as needed."

Erin looked up from her newspaper and scowled. "I think not."

"Worth a shot," Angie chuckled.

CHAPTER 18

When the snow melted with the coming of spring, Hannah called Mom and me together and asked us if we wanted to see her pond. She bundled us into the old pickup truck she kept in the barn and drove us on an old two-track drive through the fields north of the house. I didn't realize Hannah owned as much land as she did.

"This property used to be farmland, but it also has some environmentally fragile wetlands that were never drained or plowed under. The previous owner was a stubborn old man in his nineties who lived alone in his farmhouse long after he couldn't take care of the place," Hannah said. "The house caught on fire when some raccoons got in the attic and chewed up the wiring. He was lucky to be rescued, but he was never going to be able to live on his own again. His family knew the property was being eagerly considered for a lakefront housing development. I came in and bought it with the promise that I wouldn't disturb the natural beauty or the wetlands. I love seeing wildlife."

The truck pulled out of the weeds and into a clearing where we could see the pond for the first time. Calling it a pond was a bit unfair. It was a small lake that was fed and drained by a creek. Hannah had added a few amenities of her own: a dock, changing room, storage shed, picnic table, and a burn pit for hosting bonfires.

"It's beautiful!" I shouted excitedly. "Do you swim here?"

"Absolutely! Nobody bothers us here except the ducks and the occasional turtle. You can tan as much as you want here and not be disturbed."

Mom sat down at the picnic table and admired the scenery. "This would make a wonderful place to write. It's inspiring!"

Hannah laughed. "I have done that a few times myself. Just check the schedule before you come out here to make sure someone else hasn't reserved it. It is also a very inspiring place for having sex, and we try not to step on each other's toes around here."

Mom glowered at Hannah but didn't say anything in reply. Robert would love the natural setting and the swimming. If we played our cards right, we might enjoy other things here in time.

Mom's divorce was finalized on the 12th of May. Chandra handed her a check for $35,000 after she'd taken her cut and paid the court expenses. She would be Christina Powell once more. Hannah asked her if there was anything she wanted to do.

"That wardrobe change you wanted to do for me. Let's go shopping!" Mom said excitedly. "I'm ready!"

Hannah nodded at Erin. "Get a schedule worked up. Take us where you think she should go. Make the reservations."

"Understood!" Erin smiled. "I'll rent the limo."

This would be our introduction to shopping Felicity Parr style. Once or twice a year, Hannah would head off to Detroit to go shopping at her favorite boutiques, spoil herself with a massage/manicure/pedicure, restock her wine cellar, and let herself be a celebrity. The boutiques knew ahead of time she'd be coming, and they'd have people specifically designated to work with her group and cater to her every whim. In return, she spent a lot of money at their establishments.

I watched my mother be reborn on that shopping trip. Dad never wanted to spend a lot of money on her. She was forbidden to wear pants—only skirts, blouses, and dresses were allowed. Hannah and her store-owner friends saw to it that my mother would lack for nothing. Her new skirts and dresses had hemlines that went no further than her knees. She bought the first pairs of jeans and pants she'd ever owned for her new role as household manager. She bought new shoes and boots. She bought a new winter coat that would keep her warm, unlike the threadbare old coat she left home with. Mom picked out two formal gowns since Hannah occasionally hosted parties at her home that would require Mom to look the part of a celebrity. Every shop we stopped at, I was also having my wardrobe upgraded. Angie gave my attendant a list of what I needed, but let me pick out my own things. Everywhere we went, Hannah introduced my mother to the owner and said, "This is my new household manager. She'll oversee our accounts with you going forward." There was pride in Hannah's voice as she spoke, and pride in my mother's face as she realized just how important a job she was being entrusted with.

At Hannah's favorite lingerie boutique, we were given proper measurements by a sweet woman named Rhonda, who had known Hannah for years. "Neither of you two have been wearing anything that fits you properly," she said. "We're going to have to totally redo your lingerie drawer. You'll look and feel so much better when we do you up properly."

"Do what you need to," Hannah said. "I'm buying."

"Tina, you come with me. We'll get you fixed up. Sharon, you take Sarah. Make her beautiful. My orders."

"Yes, ma'am!" Sharon said. "Practical or sexy?" she asked me.

"Can I do both?"

"Of course!" she smiled.

I looked over at Angie. "Are you coming?"

She smiled and shook her head. "I have shopping of my own to do. Besides, I might want to be surprised someday." With that, she set out on her own, leading me to wonder what she meant.

Sharon helped me pick out the things I wanted. I was never going to be frumpy again. I wanted to be beautiful, even if no one was going to see what I was wearing. Besides bras and panties, I wanted to have some camisoles, hosiery for formal dresses, and an extra pair of pajamas. I was ready to do a fitting to make sure everything was perfect when something on a mannequin caught my eye. It was a red lace housecoat and matching panties. I stared at it, entranced.

"Save that for your wedding night," Mom said. "You're way too young to look at that!" She had finished her selections and was heading off to be fitted as well.

"Let's both get one!" I said excitedly.

"Sarah, what on Earth would I do with it?"

"One day, you're going to meet someone who will love you the way you should have been loved, and I want them to see how beautiful you are on your first night together."

"She's right, you know," Rhonda said softly.

"I'm going to save mine for the right person, too. Let's do this for ourselves and not for anyone else."

Mom sighed. "I must be crazy. Do you have this in blue?"

"Absolutely, Tina."

"I want the red!" I said proudly.

We had our fittings as Rhonda and her tape measure were true to form. I heard Mom call my name from one of the other fitting booths, and I turned to Sharon. "Is it safe to see her? I'm not dressed."

Sharon stuck her head outside the room. "It's safe. Second door to your left."

I scurried over wearing one of the new bra and panty sets I'd bought. It was a little provocative, but not the worst thing I'd chosen. I knocked, and Rhonda opened the door. Mom was wearing the blue housecoat and panties I'd talked her into buying. You could see her breasts through the fabric. She looked so beautiful and sexy.

"Your father would never have allowed this," she said quietly, admiring herself in the mirror.

"Dad never deserved you," I said.

"I like this," she said to herself.

"This is who we should be," I said, putting my arm around her. "We were meant to shine."

We had a wonderful time getting spoiled at the spa afterwards. Hannah added an extra stop at her jeweler to get Mom a couple necklaces and some earrings she could wear with her formal gowns. The wine shop we stopped at was given Hannah's restocking needs. They had a special import license that allowed Hannah to get things from overseas that she enjoyed and wouldn't normally be able to get. Being rich has its privileges, and Hannah insisted on the best alcohol. She was a wine snob and proud of it. We ate dinner in Detroit and had the limo take us back home. The limo driver earned a thousand-dollar tip that day for putting up with us and all our shopping bags.

One more thing remained on Hannah's agenda. "You know what I would love to do before bed? Bust open a bottle of good champagne, fire up the hot tub, and toast your new life as Tina Powell. Shame you don't drink."

Tina smiled. "I'll repent later. Tonight, I'll join you."

"I wasn't expecting a yes!" Hannah hugged Tina. "Just one glass, though. I don't fancy dragging you all the way over to the other wing of the house."

"Hey, Tina," Erin said. "As long as you're going to repent anyway, how about we skinny dip in the hot tub? No guys around tonight."

Mom laughed at this. "Nice try, but I'm still sober."

That night was special. Somewhere in her past, Mom had snuck a glass of champagne or two when she was in college. She knew she liked it, and she found it was as good as she remembered. Mom and Erin allowed Angie and me to have champagne as well, even though we were underage. It was a special occasion, and special occasions sometimes required the bending of rules. I discovered I had my mother's fondness for champagne as well. Mom wound up having three glasses, and she was starting to get buzzed.

"Do you want to skinny dip now?" Erin teased her.

Mom met the suggestion with a silly grin. "I'm already off the wagon. May as well. Are we all going to do it?"

"I don't see why not. This is just as much about Sarah's liberation as it is yours. Do you want to, Sarah?" Hannah asked.

"Do it!" Angie shouted. "I dare you!"

"I'm in!" I shouted.

I learned that women who skinny-dip should be careful when standing next to water jets. I will never live that error of judgment down. Angie mimics the moan I made now and then just to tease me. I also learned just how beautiful Angie is. She's spellbinding. I tried not to look at her, but I couldn't help myself. She knew I was staring. She made no secret of the fact that she was admiring me. There was only one thing to do about it. I dunked her. She dunked me back, and Hannah scolded us for splashing them. We had to behave the rest of the evening, even though neither of us wanted to, and both of us knew it.

Mom spent a good hour in her chapel the next morning trying to repent before she gave up and settled on mopping the floors as penance. From that day forward, she always had a glass of wine with her dinner and one before bed. When Hannah asked her about it, Mom simply replied, "Wine tastes better than tears."

***

March turned into May. I turned fifteen and had my very first real birthday party with actual friends. I could be as noisy as I wanted to, dance to my heart's content, and have Robert hold my hand under the table when no one was looking. I didn't need anything special. My shopping trip had totally spoiled me. I told my friends to get me simple, inexpensive things that would be practical or remind me of them. Lucy sketched a caricature of Robert and me. Yuki gave me a Sailor Moon figurine. Robert made a mixtape of his favorite songs that reminded him of me. Angie and Kelcee got me a vibrator. I shrieked when I opened it, and my friends broke out laughing.

"You said you wanted something practical and that would remind you of us," Kelcee said with a sly smile. "I'd say we did both." Angie still hadn't been able to stop laughing and couldn't talk.

"Where did you even get that thing?" Lucy giggled. "I thought you had to be a certain age to shop in places that sold sex toys?"

Joey raised his hand. "I'm old enough. They gave me a shopping list."

Robert was sitting beside me, laughing with Brian and Dan. Yuki was whacking Kelcee and Angie with a couch cushion. Then everyone settled down, and it was as if nothing had happened.

"Wait a second," I said in disbelief. "How is it my mother hasn't run in here and confiscated it yet?"

Dee smiled. "We bribed Hannah to keep your mother busy for a while. Go hide that thing now!"

I grabbed it and ran to my bedroom. When I returned, I asked the question I'd been pondering as I was charging from one end of the house to the other. "All of you knew. Even the guys?"

Everyone nodded. It was Melanie who spoke up. "Our parents aren't the only ones with sex drives. All of us ladies have them."

Dan's face twitched when she said that, but Melanie didn't see it. Melanie never looked at him when she truly needed to, and it was starting to bother me.

Mom arranged for the two of us to have a separate birthday get-together with both sets of my grandparents, the first time any of them had seen us in person since we escaped. She made it clear that we would continue to keep our whereabouts hidden for the time being, just to be safe. Dad hadn't threatened us directly, but he wasn't behaving well in jail and wasn't emotionally stable. Grandpa Brenner told us this himself. Daniel Brenner's bitterness and hatred were consuming him, and none of us at that table were looking forward to him getting out. Because he wasn't behaving, he wasn't getting time taken off his sentence. He had managed to get another month tacked on for his troubles.

Angie turned seventeen on May 27th. Erin bought her a used but very sharp Jeep that would get her to and from school safely in all kinds of weather. Angie was incredibly excited about it and deeply thankful. For as mischievous as Angie could be, she had always been responsible driving on her learner's permit with Erin beside her. She was ready to take the next step in life. Joey passed his final exams with flying colors and was waiting for his acceptance letter from Michigan Tech. Kelcee was not ready to let Joey go. It became painfully obvious that she loved him more than Angie did, and Joey loved her more than he realized. Angie understood the situation and stepped back a bit to let them spend more time together.

Melanie and Yuki approached me during one of our study sessions and asked for a private chat. I asked whether Robert could be present, and they agreed without hesitation.

"We are going to continue our study group during the summer," Yuki said. "Not every day. Maybe once or twice a week, for whoever can come. We want to prepare for the classes we'll be taking in the fall, so we have a jump on everyone else and don't forget anything we learned this year."

"We'd like your mom to help us. She's got ties to the PTA that might get the help we need. I want to make sure we stay at the top of our class and don't fall behind," Melanie added.

Robert sighed. "That would give you an unfair advantage over everyone else. They'll never agree to that."

"They can do something!" Melanie whined.

"I'll ask," I said. "But who wants to hang out and do homework in the summer other than you?"

"You have a pond," Melanie said. "My sister's told me all about it. Sounds like the perfect place to hang out and have fun **after** we do our homework!"

"I thought you didn't want Dan to see you in a bikini!" I laughed.

Melanie blushed. "It's summer vacation. We're not taking tests, so I suppose I can relax a bit. You want to show off for Robert, right?"

"I wouldn't mind. I think you'd both look great." Robert was never shy about speaking his mind, and Melanie blushed even more at this. I wondered if she had a crush on him.

"I suppose," I drawled. "Will we be wearing swimsuits or skinny dipping?"

Melanie gave me a playful kick in the shins. "Hello! I'm not my sister!"

"I thought you were better than that!" Yuki protested, staring at me directly.

"I need to sell this to Mom. She already knows what Angie and her bunch like to do there," I said. "I have to persuade her we intend to be on our best behavior."

"Nice try, but you'd totally strip. Angie's messed with your brain," Yuki muttered.

"I am not ready to do that in front of a guy yet," I said sternly. "When the time comes, however, I'm not going to hold back. If my husband treats me right, he gets to see all of me, and I'll love showing it all to him. That's how marriage is supposed to work, right?"

"My parents drink sake and watch television," Yuki shrugged. "Maybe they'll play dominoes if they're really feeling frisky."

Melanie shrugged. "It's hard to be passionate with kids in the house. Not that I don't hear my folks doing it now and then. Usually it's my sister, though. I can't believe my parents let her fuck in the house!"

"My parents do it twice a week," Robert said.

Melanie and Yuki both made horrified faces. "I don't want to think of your dad having sex! He's my teacher!" Melanie groaned.

Robert shrugged. "They're talking about whether they want to try for another kid. Mom's in her forties, and there's some risk involved with pregnancies at that age. I think she wants to try anyway."

Melanie looked thoughtfully at me. "We could do a women's study day now and then and not invite the boys. Then we could lose the swimsuits, right?"

Yuki shook her head. "You'll make the rest of our classmates jealous. You know that, right? If we make ourselves more noticeable, we put a bigger target on ourselves than we already have."

"I get it," Melanie said. "But I don't want to live my whole life in fear of what other people think. I want to be an attorney, and attorneys are tough. If I can't handle someone who doesn't like that I'm tanned in places they aren't, how the hell do I stand up in court and face off with my client's life and well-being potentially at stake?"

"Let me get permission first, and then we'll see about that," I said. That was good enough for the two of them, and they left Robert and me alone.

I walked over and hugged him. "Not many more days before we can date," I whispered to him.

"I know," he said. "I can't wait." He paused and looked down at his feet. "I'll try to be that guy for you. I'll try to treat you right."

"I know you will. That's why I intend to say yes. Do you plan on making me regret that?"

"No," he said firmly.

"Good answer." I kissed him on the cheek. "I love you."

"I love you too," he whispered.

"We heard that!" Yuki called out. "Don't make us tell Mr. Hill you're cheating!"

He paused and gave me one of those smiles of his. "Are you really going skinny dipping in that pond?"

"Play your cards right, and you might find out," I teased him, and then we returned to join our friends and finish studying.

Mom investigated Melanie's request with the school. She was able to get them to send home textbooks and some instructional materials so we could be a little more prepared, but that's all they would do. Teachers wanted to teach their material in their own way, after all. Kelcee decided to try teaching us anything we couldn't figure out ourselves.

Miss Reimer cornered me after class shortly after the request was made. "Your mother says you might be interested in a career as an author. You should write regularly as part of your daily activities. I hope to see you in my creative writing class someday."

"Why is Mom talking about that?" I asked.

"Because she asked me if I'd read some of her stuff. I'm going to coach her over the summer and see if she's any good. I wouldn't mind looking at anything you might submit as well. I'll be honest with what I see, so don't turn in anything half-assed."

"Thank you," I said. "I might do that. You and Mom are really getting along well. I'm glad."

Miss Reimer gave me an enigmatic smile. "Your mom is fascinating. She's trying so hard to make sense of the new world she's been dropped into, and I'm amazed she's keeping her head above water. It's nice to have someone with similar interests. I haven't had that since I graduated."

CHAPTER 19

There came an afternoon in the first week of June that was too dreadfully warm to be stuck in class. Nobody wanted to be in school that day, and everyone was looking forward to summer break once exams were over the next week. Robert waited with me for my mom to pick us up after school. He'd abandoned his jeans for the comfort of his gym shorts. Mom was usually there when school let out, but she was a bit late today, and we sat in the shade of a tree waiting for her.

By now, our relationship was the worst-kept secret at school. Everyone knew we were unofficially dating. We weren't very good at hiding it, either. We'd realize we were holding hands and then quickly let go and hope no one noticed. South Lyon High School politely yawned and looked the other way. Even the principal simply asked us if we were practicing for summer vacation when she caught us one day. We quickly nodded with embarrassment and slunk away. Once we were in the comfort of Mom's backseat, we cuddled up next to each other as much as the seatbelts would allow and held hands.

I'd mentioned the existence of our pond to Robert, and I decided to walk out there with him on this warm afternoon. That proved to be a great decision. The walk through the fields allowed Robert to show off the science his father had taught him through the years. He pointed out the meadowlarks and bluebirds singing to us and the kinds of flowers and grass that were growing in the field, and what they provided to the ecosystem.

"Did your aunt mean to let the farmland revert to its natural state?" he asked me.

"I don't know exactly what she planned, but she's very conservation-oriented. She loves seeing the wildlife outside her windows, and preserving the land as it is now makes her happy."

"I need to bring Dad out here," Robert said with glee. "There are some bird calls I don't recognize because they aren't common in these parts. Having this much grassland existing intact is rare in this part of Michigan. You're blessed. That's why so many creatures are excited to be living here."

I smiled. "Ask before you do it, though. The last thing I need to have happen is for him to come wandering through the field with his butterfly net and find Angie and Kelcee having sex with Joey out here."

Robert laughed. "I bet that actually happens, doesn't it?"

"You know it. She's already warned me to be careful wandering up here without asking her plans first. And yes, I checked. They aren't home."

Robert fell in love with the pond as soon as he saw it. Before I could even stop him, he had his shoes off and was knee deep in the water, looking around for turtles and frogs. The ducks were not amused and were angrily chiding him for disturbing their peace. This was Robert to his core: he wanted to explore the world. He'd be a fine teacher or scientist with the Department of Natural Resources.

I went into the supply cabinet and pulled out a couple of beach blankets to lie down on the grass. Eventually, he rejoined me on the shore. We lay down beside each other and held hands, admiring the clouds and watching the birds circle overhead.

"This is going to sound dumb," he said. "I think I could get used to this. I wish we could be like this forever."

"How is that dumb?" I asked in reply. "That's exactly how I feel, too!"

"If I were thinking rationally, I'd say we are going to grow up and go away to college. Our lives might well take us in completely different directions."

"That's a good possibility," I said thoughtfully. "That's why we need to enjoy where we are now. Live in the moment and savor every bit of happiness because it is so special. If it comes to pass that we are still doing this when we're eighty, we'll rejoice in these memories. If we part, always remember that this is what life is supposed to be like. Let's find partners who give us the chance to live that dream."

"Right now, I can only think about you," he replied, squeezing my hand.

"How cold is the water?"

"Way too soon for swimming," he said, trying to read my mind.

"Damn. We have this place all to ourselves. Shame we can't exploit it."

"This is fine," he said. "I'm happy. But you'd totally jump in there naked, wouldn't you?"

"Hell, yes!" I laughed. "It's hot out here! If I did, would you join me?"

Robert suddenly found himself contemplating an interesting summer vacation.

***

It was the Sunday night before exams started. I'd been studying for three hours and felt I was ready to go for tomorrow's tests. I figured I would relax for an hour before bed and slipped my headphones on to listen to some music and decompress. I closed my eyes and was lost in my own little world until I felt the mattress bounce. I had company. I opened my eyes and shut off the music. "Studying done?"

"I hate exams," Angie sighed. "My brain feels like it is going to explode." She stretched out on the bed and felt around for a pillow. She chuckled to herself. "Should have brought mine along."

"You plan on sleeping here or something?" I asked her. I took off my headphones and set them aside.

"Wouldn't your mother love that!" She looked over at me and smiled. "You excited yet? Wednesday's the day."

"A little. I have to pass my exams first before I get too excited."

"You aren't going to fail. I think you can let yourself daydream a little. Are you going to kiss him?"

"Of course I'm going to kiss him. I can finally do it legally now. We've been cheating all this time!" I readjusted the position of my pillow so the two of us could share it and Angie could be more comfortable. Angie readily snuggled up beside me.

"Do you really believe what you said the other day about true love?" she asked me.

"Without a doubt," I replied.

"And is Robert it?"

"I have no way of knowing yet. Ask me after we've dated for a while. If he isn't, someone else will come along. I'm just going to take life as it comes and deal with it."

"I wish I did. I lost all that childish optimism by junior high."

"Why? Was it because of your dad?"

"My dad wrecked so much of my childhood, but Mom and I did get away from him, and I was ready to make a new start. We moved in here, things settled down, we learned how to be normal again, and I found I adored Hannah. I wanted to be just like her when I grew up. I fell in love with her when I was twelve. I tried to explain to her how I felt, and she told me that it could never work out with me being so young and her being an adult. I vowed I'd get older, be an adult myself one day, and ask her again. She knew how I felt. She knew…and yet she turned around and started sleeping with my mom…"

Good God, can any of the Brenner family not wreck every relationship they touch? Grandpa and Grandma ruined their children. Dad ruined Mom and me. Hannah cluelessly ruined Angie. I'm getting ready to start a relationship with Robert, and I am in love with Angie, too. I'm no better. I drew Angie into a tight embrace. "I'm sorry. She's my aunt and all, but that was a shitty thing to do to you."

"She was my hero. I decided I was going to be like her. I wasn't going to give a shit either. I'd date who I wanted, fuck who I liked, and I would never look back. At least Joey and Kelcee kept me sane, but they won't be around forever, and I don't know what happens after they go. I'm scared."

"You're an amazing person," I said. "Don't sell yourself short. Don't sell them short, either. They've been with you through too much not to care deeply about you. They need to figure things out, and that might take time. You'll have Kelcee for your whole senior year, and I'm sure Joey will come home a few times. I'll be here with you, too. I promise that."

"You will?"

"I promise." I leaned over and gently kissed her.

"Now you need to promise me something in exchange. I want to hang out with you and Robert when we can this summer. Let's see how we get along. If we really hit it off well and I don't get back together with Kelcee and Joey, would you at least consider the three of us being together?"

"Shit! What did you say?" I was in disbelief.

"You heard me. I am falling in love with both of you." Angie sighed. "You were so lost and adorable when you first walked in here. I thought it would be fun to teach you the ropes, make you a little more daring, and flirt with you a bit. I didn't expect this to happen."

I hugged her. "I'm enjoying it. I didn't expect this either. So, we see if there's a spark between the three of us? Isn't that you cheating on your partners?"

"What is this time of our lives about if not trying to find the best partner or partners? If my thing with Kelcee and Joey doesn't work out, I should be able to choose someone else."

She had a point. Robert and I might never get to the place we dreamed of. Maybe it could be someone different. There was nothing wrong with keeping my options open, was there? "If I ever did date two people, it wouldn't be like your group."

She smiled curiously at me. "What's the end game then? Joey, Kelcee, and I were just in it for fun. What do you want?"

"In twenty years, you and I getting served breakfast in bed by our husband and our children. That would make me happy. My mom never got that once."

Angie put her hand on my cheek and stroked it gently. "If only life really worked that way."

"It never will if you aren't willing to at least try." The ridiculousness of my saying that hit me as soon as it left my mouth. I meant it about her relationships. I didn't mean it for myself. Did I? That was a hell of a Freudian slip.

Angie smiled her most mischievous smile. "Gotcha!"

"That's not what I meant, and you know it!" I pounced on Angie and began tickling her. After we finished, a thought occurred to me. "Robert's going to freak out. He'll never say yes. Never in a million years."

"Is that what you think? Robert and Joey talk to each other. He sees how close you and I are. He asked Joey if anything was going on between us."

"And what did Joey tell him?"

"If nothing is happening, you have nothing to worry about. If there is, date them both and see who is most serious about whom. If nobody wants to leave, you have double the fun. I had a great three years. Maybe you'll have an amazing life."

I wonder what Robert thought of that.

***

The last day of school came, and it was hard to concentrate on my exams, knowing what was waiting for me at the end of my final class. When the dismissal bell rang, I walked outside and headed for the flagpole. Robert was there waiting for me with his father, my mother, and most of our friends. I found the whole idea suddenly becoming ridiculous. I think Robert did, too.

"Geez, he's just going to ask me out! It's not that big a deal!" I sighed.

"It is for me," Robert said.

"I hope so!" I laughed. "The sooner you ask me, the sooner everyone goes home!"

Mom and Mr. Hill got their cameras ready. The two of us looked at everyone sheepishly.

"Thank God you didn't tell anyone when you asked me out," Lucy said to Brian.

"You could all just leave us alone, you know," I shouted at her.

"Where would the fun in that be? We have boring lives," Melanie said. "Make us all happy."

"We're ready," Mom said.

"You're no longer my student, Miss Powell. Go for it," Mr. Hill said.

Robert gently put his arms around me and softly kissed me. "I'm ready. Want to be my girlfriend?"

"Yes!" I shouted and kissed him back. We hugged after that, and then everyone came over to wish us the best. We'd invested so much time and energy into thinking about this moment for a whole semester, and now it was over in the blink of an eye.

Joey had graduated and was working, so he wasn't there. Kelcee and Angie were. They hung back for a bit to let others offer their best wishes first. Mom and Mr. Hill were off talking with the principal and weren't keeping an eye on us, and that's when they came over to greet us.

"We are so double-dating each other this summer," Kelcee said excitedly.

"That and swimming at the pond," Angie added, giving off a devious smile.

"Do you think he'd mind?" Kelcee asked. "What do you think, Sarah? Robert could put suntan oil on all of us. He's a gentleman, right?" She shot Robert a mischievous glance.

"Who is going to take care of me?" came his playful reply. He seemed to guess exactly what she was thinking and decided to play along with the joke.

"That would be your girlfriend's job. Of course, if she doesn't mind us helping…"

"And what would Joey say about that?" Robert teased.

"Don't get them all pregnant at once," Angie whispered in his ear.

Robert blushed. He wasn't ready for that yet, and he knew it. The two of them laughed uproariously and walked off together.

"Stick with me. I'm much easier to deal with," I said.

He pulled me into an embrace and kissed me warmly. Our final kiss at the flagpole lasted longer than the first two. There was a little bit of tongue involved—then a little bit more.

"Sarah! That's enough!" Mom shouted.

Robert and I smiled at each other. This was going to be an amazing summer.

CHAPTER 20

Our families had wanted to celebrate our decision to become a couple by getting together for dinner. Mr. Hill had wanted to have the meal at their place, but Robert had been begging him to come visit the pond, and so it wound up at ours instead. Angie drove us out to the pond. Surprisingly, she stayed and joined the tour. Mr. Hill fell in love with the place immediately. It took no time at all for father and son to start wading in the shallows, hunting for fish and amphibians, and talking about how the ecosystem the pond was part of worked. Mr. Hill already had ideas for plants and animals that might be in the area that we should be searching for, and ways to preserve the habitat for the future. Watching Robert and his father discuss science was amazing. What I wasn't prepared for was Angie taking an interest in their discussions. It wasn't long before she was in the water with them, poking around and asking questions. Mr. Hill seemed taken aback at first, but soon welcomed her into the discussion. I felt left out, so I joined them. We all had an impromptu science lesson that afternoon that was truly enjoyable.

As we drove back to the house for dinner, Mr. Hill remarked to Angie. "You showed more interest in science today than the entire year I had you in my class!"

"I didn't think I liked science that much. It's different when you can see and touch at the same time as you hear the lecture. Things are more real to me that way."

"How is it you have two partners who are future engineers and not love science?" I teased her. "Doesn't that make conversation boring?"

She flashed me with a wicked smile. "Thankfully, they like sex as much as they like science. I always know how to make the conversation more interesting if it gets boring."

"Hello! There's a teacher in the back seat!" I reminded her.

"I'm used to her," Mr. Hill said. "She deliberately tries to yank my chain. I had to learn not to react to everything she said. It was hard. She could be very funny."

"Trying to get you to laugh was part of the fun," Angie giggled.

"I'm a bit skeptical that you've suddenly converted to loving science. What's really going on here?"

"I doubt I'm ever going to love it as much as you and your son do, but I should know something about what Robert loves if I'm going to be his friend. If he and Sarah have kids, you can bet there will be little science nerds running around. Aunt Angie is going to have to babysit. Gotta step up my science game either way."

She was improvising this, the wench! She wasn't lying. She wanted to be interested in things Robert liked because she was exploring the idea of what it would be like to date him. She was a demon playing chess with us as her pieces. I wasn't just a pawn, however. In my own way, I was playing the game as her opponent, trying to beat her and make her submit to me. This was like one of Aunt Hannah's novels, except that I was living it.

"You aren't thinking of having kids any time soon, I hope?" Mr. Hill asked his son.

"No, Dad! Geez, why did you have to freak him out like that, Angie?"

Angie gave a cheery laugh. "If I wanted to freak him out, I'd ask him how he felt if you and I had kids someday."

"I think I would ask Tina how to become a Christian. Your children would bring on the apocalypse." Angie thought this was the funniest joke he'd ever told.

By the time we'd arrived back at the house, it was a little past six o'clock. We walked into the house and found everyone waiting for us in the parlor and happily chatting among themselves.

"Hey, you!" Mrs. Hill said to her husband as we walked in. "I was wondering when you were going to show up."

"We were out touring the grounds," Mr. Hill said, sauntering over and giving his wife a kiss. "Lots of fish and turtles to see!"

She laughed. "As you can see, being a science teacher cramps Jerry's style a bit. Give him a field or a lake to explore, and he's in his true element."

"If that's what you love the most, why didn't you do that for a living instead of dealing with us?" Angie asked.

"I thought about it," Mr. Hill said. "I really did. But that would mean I'd be away from Brenda again, and I couldn't bear that after four years of college. I took a teacher's job so we could get married and be together. I've never regretted choosing her, even if that means I am stuck dealing with you."

Brenda stood up and gave her husband a hug and a surprisingly affectionate kiss, given the situation. "Twenty-six years of marriage and no regrets here," she said, her eyes beaming happily at him.

"Have your parents always been like this?"

"They do fight now and then, but never for long. Most of the time, they're happily in love. That's what I want my life to be like."

My hand clutched his. That's what I wanted, too—nothing like what Mom endured. I just wanted to love and be loved. Just for a moment, I felt a hand slide along the curve of my butt. Angie was adding her own opinion on the matter.

Mom decided it was time we sat down to eat and herded us into the dining room. The conversation continued in there over dinner as we got to know each other better. Brenda was a chemical engineer who worked in Ford's research labs in Dearborn. She was working on fuel emissions for vehicles, trying to make cars and trucks pollute less. The subject of my courtship with Robert came up. Apparently, the adults were going to discuss what rules we were required to follow afterward. We just wanted to hang out as much as we could and get to know each other better. I could live with restrictions.

"I do notice Sarah tends to talk seriously about Robert in a way I never thought about with boys when I was their age," Mom said.

Mr. and Mrs. Hill gazed knowingly at each other. "It was that way with us when we were in school," she said. "The two of us weren't allowed to date officially until we were sixteen, but we had been a couple since we were thirteen. Since we lived next door to each other and had been best friends since we were in second grade, splitting us up was too hard for our parents, and they never really succeeded. They certainly went out of their way to make it tough on us. That was something we vowed we would never repeat with our kids."

"I never loved anyone else," Mr. Hill said proudly. "I know that's not normal, and I've told Robert not to expect that his romantic life will be like ours. He has our permission to take his own path in life as long as he is smart and can justify his actions."

Robert was sitting between myself and Angie. He perked up when his dad spoke. "I've never felt this way about a person before, and have it mean something. I like things few people my age enjoy, and that makes getting to know people a challenge. Sarah can look at those things and appreciate them in a way no one else ever has. We're not going to be just like you and mom. We're going to be something very different, I think."

"Grant us the grace to let us find our way," I added, casting a glance at Robert and Angie.

"As long as you prove to us you're responsible, that shouldn't be a problem," Mrs. Hill said.

"Angie, what's your future like now that Joey is going to be leaving in a couple months?" Mr. Hill asked.

"Dating Kelcee for a year before she leaves. Then I guess I'll see what happens after that."

"Kelcee's been poring over her scholarship options. All of us in the science department are trying to help her. We're pretty sure she can get into Michigan Tech on her own, but it would be nice to make it easier for her. She's always been one of our best students in the department. Even better than Joey, in my opinion."

I thought I detected some unease in Angie when he said that. Robert did, too. He discreetly put a hand on her leg for a moment to comfort her. She quietly took his hand and held it— only for a few seconds, but it was enough. Mrs. Hill saw it. I thought I detected a hint of a smile.

"They're going to the same university, right?" Mrs. Hill asked.

"Yes, that's the plan," Angie said.

"Where are you going to school after you graduate?"

"Haven't thought about it. Not really in any hurry. I'll probably just work for Hannah in some capacity."

"You aren't freeloading off us," Erin said sternly. "If you don't get a job this summer, we will be putting you to work around the house."

"Angie, you have good grades. You shouldn't sell yourself short," Hannah replied. "What do you want to do with your life?"

"I'm thinking porn star," Angie giggled. "Just kidding! Just kidding, Mom!"

Erin was horrified. Hannah was trying not to laugh. Mom glared at her.

"I think I'd like to have children someday," Angie said in a more serious voice.

"I want to as well," I said.

"We'll deal with it when we need to," Robert said. He promptly continued eating as if nothing unusual had happened.

"Which won't be for a very long time, if ever." Mom said. "Do I make myself clear?"

"Yes, ma'am," he said quickly.

I blushed a bit. "Let's see how the summer goes before you worry about that," I mumbled.

Angie was giggling. "How are you ever going to make it through high school, you two?"

"I'll tell your teachers to give you lots of homework," Mr. Hill said. "That will keep you busy and out of trouble."

"Never stopped us," Angie said with an evil smile. "We've done homework in bed after sex lots of times."

"Mr. Hill could have done without that visual," Erin sighed. From the pained expression he wore, she was very much correct.

"If Kelcee goes to school with Joey, doesn't that mean they plan on continuing the relationship?" Brenda asked.

"If Joey doesn't find someone in the interim, maybe. At our age, there aren't any guarantees in life. We had a great three years. If it goes longer, that's wonderful. If it doesn't, no regrets."

"I could never live like that," Robert said thoughtfully.

"Nor I," I added.

Mrs. Hill observed the three of us intently. "Of course, you could always date Robert and Sarah. I have the sneaking suspicion they wouldn't mind."

Mr. Hill coughed on his dinner and looked over at his wife. "Don't encourage them!"

We giggled nervously. Brenda smiled. "The three of you have an interesting vibe. You're more than friends, even if you don't realize it yet. I'm curious what you'll become."

Mom looked at me. "But you just started dating Robert today. You like boys."

"I love Robert very much. I care for Angie deeply. I don't know what that means. None of us does. For right now, I'm happy with my boyfriend, and I don't plan on leaving him."

"A wise answer," Hannah said. "Take your lives one day at a time, and don't listen to adults who have weird ideas while drinking." She cast a stern glance at Brenda Hill.

"So, I should ignore you then?" Angie asked Hannah.

"At your peril."

***

After dinner, the three of us went off to Angie's room to borrow her stereo and listen to music. We were waiting to see what our parents would decide. In the end, the results weren't bad.

"I expect you two to be home from any date by 9 PM unless you have special permission otherwise," Mom said. "If you have a parent with you, that can go to 11 PM. No drugs or alcohol, period. If the cops call us, you'd better have saved someone from drowning or rescued a cat out of a tree."

"You are free to hold hands and kiss all you want. Keep the grown-up kisses to yourself. We don't want to see those!" Mr. Hill said.

"We enjoy camping during the summer," Mrs. Hill said. "You've never been camping in your life according to your mother. Sarah, you are invited to come with us this year."

"Camping?" I asked. "You're letting me go camping with you?"

"Why not?" Mrs. Hill said. "You don't think you'd like it?"

"I think I'd love it, actually! Will there be swimming and campfires and stuff?"

"And canoeing. We canoe a lot in the summer," Robert said. "I told my folks they should ask if you wanted to come."

"I do!" I hugged him. "That sounds like so much fun! Thank you!"

"Beginning Monday, you'll be splitting time working for Tina and me, learning the operations of the house and the basics of being a publicist and agent," Erin said sternly. "You'll be paid for your time. You will be expected to sit in on the summer study sessions the group is planning as well."

"Aww, Mom!" Angie whined.

Mr. Hill looked over at Robert. "You have a summer job as well. Three days a week, I want you over here to do an ecological study on Hannah's property. I want a general outline of the different kinds of habitats, plants, and animals, and the potential problems you might encounter. I want everything mapped out and photographed. Hannah will lend you a room in the basement, which you can use as an office."

"Sounds like fun. I'm down for it."

"Sarah, you can visit the Hills a minimum of once a week when there are adults home," Mom said. She took a deep breath. "This is hard for me. I expected you to be a child for a while longer. I'm very uncomfortable with how fast you are growing up."

Mrs. Hill took my mom's hand, helping her regain her composure, and said, "She wants you to be safe. All of us do. Telling you not to have sex until you're older is the smart thing to do, but teenagers in love can do things no matter what we as parents tell you. Jerry and I had our first time when we were your age. If things do happen and you feel like you may need to get contraceptives or birth control, don't be afraid to ask for help. Even if it isn't us—ask someone."

"I've seen young women at school get pregnant. I had one in my class a few years ago. That's heartbreaking. That changes your life permanently. Neither of you wants to be a parent this young. Make good choices." Mr. Hill turned to us. "Anything you'd like to say in response?"

"We intend to make good choices," I said. "You have my word on that. Thank you for believing in us. We're nowhere near ready for sex."

"We'll believe in you as long as you keep giving us reasons to believe," Mom said. "If you break our trust, you'll get a different response. I'm proud of my daughter. They're proud of you, Robert. That's how we're going to proceed."

"You need to get things worked out on your side," Erin said. "It's not fair to Joey and Kelcee to do it any other way."

"Understood," Angie said.

"One last thing," Mrs. Hill said with a smile. "As of now, we can cease the formalities. Call us Jerry and Brenda when we're together outside of school. That goes for you, too, Angie. I have a feeling you'll be part of the family before too long."

***

When it came time for Robert to go home, I kissed him goodnight. Angie hugged him for a long time and whispered something in his ear that I couldn't hear. Whatever it was made him blush and made her laugh. I asked her about it, of course. I had to.

"I like it up the ass."

I shook my head. "How do I compete with that?"

"You don't, silly. You learn at your own pace when the time is right. There was never a competition between Kelcee and me for Joey. If she's out there tonight fucking him, I'm happy for her. We love him, and we love each other. Maybe one day, I'll love you, and we'll love Robert."

"And we'll grow old and happy together. What a weird future that would be. It could never happen. Could it?"

"The fact you're thinking about it should tell you it isn't impossible. Not at all. It's already happened once. Why couldn't it happen again?"

There was a simple solution to this. "I kissed Lucy, and I didn't become attracted to her. Maybe I should kiss you and prove to myself this whole idea is stupid."

"I'm right here. Do it."

155

I kissed her. It felt so much different than the time I kissed Lucy. I could hear my heart pounding. I could feel the softness of her lips and the warmth of her body as I embraced her. She kissed me back. I held her tighter and kissed her once more. I opened my eyes and saw her hunger staring back at me. I felt her tongue sliding between my lips. I let it in. We began kissing furiously. I needed to take a breath.

"That's enough for one night," she said. "Still want to claim you aren't attracted to me?"

"What do I do now? What about Robert?"

"You go on loving him as you always have."

"But I just cheated on him! With my best friend!"

"Nope. Not even close. What you did do was prove to yourself you're not like everyone else. You could be happy with either sex if it came to it. What if you could have both? The best of both worlds. That's what I've had for three years, and I've loved every minute of it. Now you need to decide what you want to do. No pressure here. I'll let you figure it out on your own. My door will always be open." With that, she ruffled my hair and shooed me out of her room.

If ever there were a moment I wished life had a do-over switch, this was the time. I'd taken a big bite from the fruit of the tree of the knowledge of good and evil, I felt as naked as Adam and Eve, and I was waiting for God to kick me out of paradise. I knew the truth about myself. Angie was right. I wasn't normal. I'd found something in myself I didn't know existed. I could pretend it didn't mean anything. I could hope it would go away. I was curious what life with Robert and Angie would be like. I knew I loved them both, and I had no idea what I should do about it now.

CHAPTER 21

The mood in the house was edgy for the next couple of days. Erin had Angie in her office answering Hannah's fan mail and cleaning out a room in the basement for Robert to use. Mom did her job as usual but retreated to her chapel when she finished work. She seemed on the verge of tears sometimes. I felt guilty. This was all due to my inability to conform to the rules of society. *If I could just love Robert, everyone would be happy. I couldn't, though. Why couldn't I? Why was I a freak like Angie and Hannah? I didn't intend this to happen.* In my head, I could hear Grandpa Brenner preaching at me. I chose to sin. My choice is negatively affecting me and the people who love me. I'm the one who needs to repent. I'm the one who needs to stay away from demons. I chose darkness over light. This is on my head.

"No!" I shouted to no one in particular. That mindset oversimplified things. My whole life has been spent watching evil things happen and have them labeled as good. Angie loved playing the part of a demon, but she was just as lost right now as I was. Somewhere in the middle of this mess was a happy medium I needed to find. I had to help her, just as she was helping me. *A demon and her exorcist…falling in love…dear God, that's the plot of a novel! That's my novel! That's what I'm meant to do with my life. I need to write that!* I ran from my room through the house, frantically looking for Hannah. I found her in the gym working out.

"Are you okay?"

"I want to write a book!" I shouted. "I know what I want to write about!"

"Tell me."

"An exorcist is sent to defeat and banish a demon, but falls in love with her instead. The demon, curious about what love feels like, spares the exorcist her life. The two of them struggle to make sense of their feelings while knowing one could kill the other at any time. They grow closer, and the demon realizes love and change are possible for her, and they forge a new path forward. They are no longer good and evil, but a healthy mixture of both." I think I may have delivered that in one long run-on sentence. I'm not sure. The words just flowed out of me like a spring bursting forth from the earth.

"I like it," Hannah said. "Go and start writing now. Write until you get stuck, then bring what you wrote to me, and I'll look at it. If that means we deliver your meals to your room, we'll do it. Erin's used to that with me when I get on writing binges. I'll tell everyone not to disturb you. You've got this! Now, go!"

I did not leave my room for three days. I couldn't stop writing. The ideas kept coming into my head, and I had to write them down for fear they would stop forever if I rested. When they did pause, I would re-read what I wrote, fix spelling and punctuation errors, and re-write parts that didn't work as well on the second read. More ideas would come. More writing would happen. The most I slept during that time was two hours. I had to follow my muse wherever it led. When I could write no more, I printed out the results and dropped them on Hannah's desk. That's the last thing I remember. Mom said I fell asleep in Hannah's chair, and they had to carry me back to my room. I slept for eighteen hours straight.

When I woke up, I stumbled into the bathroom and took a shower. After I got out, I threw on a bathrobe and made myself a pot of coffee. Mom must have heard the shower running because she knocked on my door soon afterwards to check on me.

"How are you feeling?" She hugged me as she asked, and I gratefully accepted it.

"Drained," I replied.

"I should think so. You gave Hannah over a hundred pages of material to read through. I'm lucky if I can write ten."

"I couldn't stop," I mumbled. "The words kept coming."

"Hannah warned me that might happen. She's had bouts of creativity like that. You ride them like a surfer rides a wave, she said. That must have been some wave."

"Did she read what I wrote?" I asked. "What did she think?"

"Hannah wants to talk to you about it. I'll let her know you're up so we can block out some time for her to do it. Miss Reimer wants to be there, too."

Now that was news. Why did my English teacher get summoned? Was it so bad that they're going to make me repeat ninth-grade English?

"Hungry?" Mom asked.

"Starving!"

"I'll bring you some food. You just stay here and relax." She left me to my thoughts and fears as I sipped my coffee.

A few minutes passed before the door burst open and a breathless Angie tumbled into the room. "I read it! I read what you wrote!"

My brain puzzled over this. "Why would you read it?"

"The demon Ashley you wrote about. She's me, isn't she? You based her on me! And Mary the exorcist is you!"

"Is it that obvious?" I asked nervously.

Angie yanked my chair away from my desk, sat down on my lap facing me, and kissed me so hard I thought I would lose consciousness. "I love it! That's the most amazing thing anyone will ever do for me as long as I live! You love me, and you're willing to write a novel because of it!"

Strictly speaking, that was not at all what I had done. At least I didn't think I had. Maybe in the blur of the creative process, those feelings spilled out. Or maybe she could read me better than I could read myself. That was potentially a very scary thing, given what she wanted to do with and to Robert and me.

"Does Robert know I'm okay?" I asked nervously.

"I told him his future wife is going to be a kick ass novelist someday. He should get used to you disappearing into your room to work like that now and then."

"Wouldn't that be something?" I hadn't quite grasped the reality of any of this yet. She kissed me again, more softly. Her tongue knocked on my lips, begging to be let in. I pulled away. "What if Mom were to walk in?"

"I told her I needed fifteen minutes to talk to you. She said she'd give me that, but not a second more. There are five loads of laundry with my name on it, and I am not going to escape that fate.”

I smiled. “Sorry about that. Kiss me again.”

She kissed me again. Angie could be a very patient teacher, and I let her lead me. I lost track of time. When it ended, I pleaded with her, “What do I do now? I want more.”

She smiled at me. “Robert’s here tomorrow. Go play tonsil hockey with him.”

“This is crazy!” It occurred to me in the moment I was still wearing my satin bathrobe. That was all I was wearing, too. In the commotion of having Angie on my lap, making out with me, the tie had begun to loosen. Everything was still covered, but only just. “It’s getting a bit drafty all of a sudden,” I whispered.

Angie looked down and giggled. “Mmm! Your mom will be back soon. What to do?” She gently let her fingers trace the contours of my body through the fabric, teasing. I was breathless.

“Look at you,” she whispered. “You are going to be a lot of fun when the time comes.”

“Too soon,” I whimpered.

She kissed me again. “Yes. But I know you want it now. When the time is right, I’m going to love being your demon. I will be yours for as long as you’ll have me.”

I took a deep breath, reached out, and softly began caressing Angie’s breasts through her shirt. I knew Angie seldom wore a bra around the house, and she’d feel pretty much the same way I felt when she was playing with me. She reacted with pleasant surprise and evident joy. "So, when the time is right, I get to play with these?" I asked.

"Only if you write me a beautiful ending."

"In real life. I love you." I kissed her softly.

"I love you too."

A thought occurred to me. "He's not going to be mad I wrote about you and not him, is he?"

Angie laughed. "God, no! You writers think alike. Hannah sat him down to clear that up right away. To quote the great Felicity Parr, 'Sarah is going to be your wife, and Angie is going to be her inspiration. The two of them are going to make you the happiest man in the world.' He's cool with that." She looked at the clock and sighed. "Duty calls. I hope your meeting with Hannah goes well."

"Yeah. Hannah and Charli."

"Charli?" She chuckled to herself. "So that's how it's going to go. Whatever works."

"What's that supposed to mean?"

"Look at it this way. Your mother is supposed to be a good Christian woman. She could put a stop to anything she didn't like at the snap of a finger. Why isn't she doing it? You know it bugs her. She said so herself. She couldn't bring herself to intervene. If Charli's coming here, she's coming here because your mother asked her to come."

"You're kidding. Mom and Charli? Why would that even happen?"

Angie smiled. "You're too new at this. Charli totally gives off lesbian vibes."

"You think?"

"I know. Kelcee and I aren't exactly part of the club, but we're friends with a few lesbians at school. We all like girls, so we can all relate to each other. Charli keeps it hidden because she doesn't want any trouble, but we know one of our own when we see her. Your mother has been living here for a while. She's getting used to being around bisexual women who cuddle each other. She knows she'll never go back to a man again after what your dad made her live through. Charli is there, being encouraging and kind and everything your dad never was, but your mother craves the most. The only thing holding her back is all the years she was told being gay was a sin. She won't stop us because she can't stop herself. When she finally lets go of the guilt, she and Charli would make a fabulous couple, even with the age difference."

It was then that we realized Mom was standing at the door and had heard every word Angie said. Both of them knew they had been found out.

"Um, Angie was just going to go do the laundry, weren't you?" I stammered.

"Yes! Right away!"

Mom stood in the doorway so she couldn't leave. "You guessed right, if that helps. Please don't tell Charli, though. I'm not ready."

Angie smiled and gave Mom a hug. "I won't say a word. You, on the other hand…is Charli even single?"

Mom thought for a moment. "I think so. I'm not sure, though."

"I'd ask her sooner rather than later. No point getting attached to something you can't have."

Mom nodded. "Good idea."

"If she is single, don't be afraid to tell her the truth. You're not sure about your feelings or where you want to go in life, but you really like her as a friend and wonder how she feels about that. She'll give you an answer. You'll roll with that."

I pulled the belt of my robe tighter. "Your demon in the book sounds a lot like your demon in real life," Mom said.

"So, I've been told," I said shyly.

"Don't make her or Robert cry, Angie. That's all I ask."

Angie hugged Mom. "You'll be amazing on your second try. Charli wants to be part of that journey you're on." Then her face suddenly changed. Something had popped into her head. "Do I get to call you Mom too at some point?"

Mom looked over at me. "What are you going to call Charli?"

"I don't know. I'll call Jerry 'Dad' for sure. I guess we'll have to ask her what she prefers if things ever get that far."

"You could call her 'Mom's new sex toy,'" Angie said with a wink.

"You can go do some laundry while I forget you said that." Mom moved out of the way, and Angie scurried out the door, laughing as she went.

***

When it came time for our conference, Hannah sat across the desk from me, while Charli sat on my right. It felt like I was before a judge with my attorney present, and I said so. The two of them smiled at each other.

"Neither of us is a professional editor," Hannah said. "I live to give my own editor headaches. Every book I write, she says the same thing. 'If you'd only write the way I want you to write, you'd make your life and mine so much easier.' I never do it."

"What did you think, though? How bad is it?" I asked nervously.

Charli took a deep breath. "This is hard for me to say because I might be your teacher again someday, and I don't want to complicate our relationship. For someone your age, it's the most incredible piece of writing I've seen as a teacher."

"For a first draft by a new author, I think it has real possibilities," Hannah said proudly. "You might have a chance at a real book if you keep working on this."

I was excited and let out a loud "Yes!"

"However, it's a first draft. Your teacher and I are going to tear it apart before your eyes. We're going to tell you what we like, what we hate, and what needs work. It needs a lot of work. I wouldn't recommend this to my editor. Not yet. But you can do this. We'll give you our advice, and you can argue with us if you disagree."

We talked for three hours. True to their word, they dissected my first attempt to the point I felt like I'd become a dead woodchuck on a highway, getting my corpse picked apart by vultures. As they did so, they taught me a writing class that I found invaluable. By the end of the night, I could understand what they were trying to tell me, and I couldn't wait to sit down and fix what was broken. I thanked them for their time. Before I left, there was one question I was dying to know the answer to.

"Why are you here, Miss Reimer? This isn't a school project. I'm not getting a grade for this. Why?"

She looked at Hannah carefully, as if seeking permission to divulge a secret. Hannah nodded. "I used to be a student at U of M once upon a time. I had your aunt as one of my professors. She was one of my references I used when I applied for my position at South Lyon."

"No way! What class?"

Charli didn't answer right away. Hannah leaned over and touched her hand softly. "Sarah can handle it. Just keep this to yourself, okay?"

"I had her for Gay and Lesbian Studies in Media," she said quietly. "I'm a lesbian."

Angie knew! "One of my friends thought you might be. You and Hannah didn't hook up, did you?"

Hannah started giggling. "Sarah, if she's not allowed to hook up with you, I certainly wasn't allowed to hook up with her. We have rules in academia, you know."

I sighed in relief. "Are you single? Someone was asking if you were. Not a student, though."

"I am. I've never found anybody I really liked who could understand me. God knows I tried in college, but I finally gave up and just decided to focus on my career."

I took a deep breath. "Someone very important to me might ask you if you'd be willing to consider her. It may be a while. She has a lot of things to work through from her last relationship. Just promise me you'll listen to her if she asks. She's a good person who deserves a lot better than life has given her."

"Let me put it to you this way, Sarah. I don't see myself dating for the foreseeable future. That does not mean I will never date again. There's someone I'm curious about now. Maybe we're thinking of the same person. If we were, and she would ask, I think I'd be very tempted to say yes. We'll see. She needs to figure things out, and I'm not going to pressure her."

"Thank you," I said, and turned to go.

"If she ever finds out you did this, Sarah…" Hannah began.

"Are you going to tell her?"

"Not a word."

"It needs to be her move. I just hope she's brave enough to make it."

CHAPTER 22

Robert didn't have a clue how he was going to proceed with the task he'd been given. Maybe that was part of the exercise. Robert had to learn how to map and inventory the same way a college student doing fieldwork would. His first day in the field was spent walking the entire eastern length of Hannah's property along the road that bordered it. He counted every tree, identified the type, and noted if it was sick or healthy. He examined the plant and animal life he saw in his walks and even found a salamander under the bridge going over the creek that ran from our pond. If he wasn't doing it right, he was at least having fun doing what he was doing. Not unlike me writing my first draft.

He arrived at the house bright and early in the morning as Mom was serving breakfast. Jerry dropped him off at the front door and left. Robert let himself in and greeted us all with a cheery "Hello!"

Erin looked around the table and sighed. "Good morning, Robert. This is what it's like first thing in the morning around here. Get used to it."

She was dressed for work. Erin and Mom were always dressed professionally at breakfast. Hannah had stumbled down from her room in a half-shirt and boxers, looking like death warmed over. Angie wore a button-down sleep shirt with the top four buttons undone. I hoped she was wearing panties underneath, but there were never any guarantees with her. Her hair was shooting off in ten different directions simultaneously. I thought Robert was coming much later, so I'd come to breakfast wearing a sports bra and athletic shorts. I hadn't touched my hair either. I wanted to crawl under the table and hide.

"Pull up a chair, Robert!" Hannah said. "Have you eaten?"

"Yes, ma'am. I'll have some coffee, though."

"Help yourself. Damn, my head hurts."

"That's your fault for drinking too much," Erin grumbled.

Robert sat down next to me and kissed me on the cheek. "Good morning, dear."

"This is awkward," I sighed.

"Nah. Mom wears a sports bra around the house a lot. It's not like I haven't seen them before."

"You haven't seen mine before! That's a big difference!"

Mom walked out of the kitchen and stopped dead in her tracks. "Your father said 9:00!"

"He decided he wanted to go fishing and changed his mind at the last minute," Robert said as he poured his coffee."

"I'll be having words with your father. Angie, button that shirt up. He doesn't get any free peeks when I'm in charge."

"What about Hannah?" Angie complained.

"Hannah, did you lose half of your shirt on the way to breakfast? Go back and find the rest of it. You're supposed to be the responsible adult who owns this place, not a Hooters waitress."

"I didn't lose it. I cut it off because Erin likes to…"

"If you complete that sentence, your next book signing will be at a Wal-Mart in Hoboken!" Erin snapped.

Angie, Robert, and I were all laughing hysterically at this point. Angie did button her nightshirt up. Hannah slunk off to dress properly. I made a dash back to my room to throw on a shirt.

Our mission for the day was to explore a clump of trees that was growing east of the pond road, surrounded by the tall grass that grew on what once were corn fields. Angie drove us out to the closest point on the two-track road, then we had to walk a few hundred yards to reach the trees. Apparently, one of the farmers who once owned the land had planted a small grove of fruit trees for their family to eat from. Two apple trees, two plum trees, a peach, a pear, and three cherry trees still survived, though they had long been neglected and had seen better days. A large pile of rocks and a couple of old tractors had been dumped there. A family of chipmunks was living in the rocks, while a grumpy groundhog had taken up residence under the stump of a dead apple tree. The hum of bees was in the air. Robert found a hive of them in an old log. All of this was within sight of the road, but we'd never bothered to notice what was there.

"It would be nice if we could save these trees," I said. "We could have fresh fruit down at the house or at least pick some to eat when we're at the pond."

"I don't know if the trees are any good," Robert said. "My dad would know who to ask, though. If they can be saved, we should try."

Angie took an interest in one apple tree, grabbed a limb, and began climbing up the trunk. She made it halfway up the tree before finding a suitable limb and settling down on it. I'd never climbed a tree before in my life. It seemed like fun, but I wasn't quite as agile as Angie.

"That tree's old. Be careful you don't fall!"

"Yes, Mom!" she called down and chucked an apple at me. "I haven't done this since I was a kid. I used to climb trees all the time to get away from all the shouting in the house. I'd get beaten for it when my dad found me, but at least I had peace for a little while."

"You don't talk about that part of your life very much," Robert said.

"I don't. It's over and done with, and I've moved on," said Angie.

Had she? I wondered about that. Burying those memories with sex, alcohol, and weed was how she coped, but she hadn't fixed a damn thing. It was all still there, waiting to burst forth and swallow her one day down the road.

"What happened to your dad?" Robert asked. "He should be in jail."

"He is. Took 'em long enough to do it, but he's locked up for thirty years. Not for beating us, though. He murdered his mother and then tried to shoot some cops. Worthless piece of shit."

"Did he ever try to find you two?" I asked.

"No. That surprised me for a while until I found out from Mom that he had a side chick. I guess if he had someone to slap around and a twelve-pack of beer a day, that was all he needed to be happy in life. We were expendable." The way her voice quivered as she spoke was notable. She and Erin had gotten out just in time, and she knew it.

We had planned to eat our lunch by the pond, but Robert decided the shade of the trees here at the grove would work just as well. Angie came down from her perch to join us, and Robert hugged her when she did. She smiled slyly and kissed him on the cheek.

"I could get used to this," she laughed.

"So could I." I kissed him and wrapped my arms around him.

"What's gotten into the two of you?" he laughed. "Did I miss the memo where I have two girlfriends instead of one?"

"You still have one. I just told her she could kiss you to see if you liked it."

Robert was briefly confused but then nodded and smiled. "Joey said something like this might happen."

"What did Joey say?" Angie asked. "I want to hear this."

"You and Kelcee were going to try and make a go of things, but if they needed a guy to help them out, I'd be perfect for the job. I like Sarah. Angie likes Sarah. Kelcee likes Angie. Everybody's happy."

Angie let out a deep sigh of frustration. "Kelcee will be very surprised to learn she's happy. Kelcee's hanging on to us for dear life now. Sometimes Joey can be very stupid for a smart guy. Take anything he says with three saltshakers and a margarita. I've half a mind to go over to his house and kick him in the nuts."

We ate our lunch and listened to music from the radio in the truck, making small talk in the process. After a while, Angie decided to liven things up in her own fashion. "Since you two wanted to ask me personal questions, I think I should get to ask you some. You each get two."

"Fair enough," Robert said. "Fire away."

"Why are you Robert and not Bob or Bobby?" Not a bad question! We had several Bobs at our school and half a dozen Bobbys, but only one Robert.

"I was Bobby until I finished second grade," he admitted. My older sister Liz said Robert sounded much more distinguished, and teachers would take me more seriously. For her education and employment, she always uses Elizabeth. She's only Liz to family and friends."

"Sarah, first question: Do you still believe in God?"

She didn't shy away with that one. "Maybe," I said. "I guess I haven't given up on the idea totally. The God I grew up believing in isn't one I want any part of. That much I do know."

"Robert, second question: If you ever dated me, what would be the scariest thing about having me as a partner?"

I thought I could guess the answer she was expecting. She thought he'd be afraid of her stealing me away from him. That wasn't what he answered, however. "Not living up to Joey and Kelcee in your eyes."

"Explain that."

"You're going from two partners who are very experienced and knowledgeable to a virgin. It would be like starting over again for you, and I'd be afraid you'd hate me for not being able to fulfill your expectations."

Angie smiled at him. "So that's how it is. Let me tell you how the world works. If I find myself in a new relationship, it is going to be a completely different dynamic from what I have now. I'm going to be learning what my partner enjoys and adjust my pace to suit theirs. It will be no different from you and Sarah learning how to please each other. That person will have to learn how to make me happy, too. That's how good relationships work. Everyone's different, and this will be a new adventure for me."

"So…what's my second question?" I asked nervously.

"We practiced some things the other day. Do you want to show Robert your new tricks today?"

I suddenly felt very shy. "I'm not sure. I was teasing him about certain things myself. I'm not ready to go that far. I want to. I just don't think I should."

"That's fair," Angie said. "If you change your mind, let me know. What was she teasing you with, Robert?"

"Skinny dipping in the pond," he said. "I've had interesting dreams since she told me that."

"For shame, Sarah! Playing with a young man's heart like that!"

"I can't help it. Talking about getting naked and doing it are two different things."

"Not in my book!" Angie hugged Robert playfully.

"Practicing what exactly?" Robert asked me.

"Umm…French kissing?"

"French kissing with a dash of groping," Angie corrected me. "I was just going to tease him a little. You offered him a whole lot more than that! Tsk-tsk!"

"I can already hear my son asking me someday, 'Dad, what did you do on your first date?' and me having to explain I got naked with his mother and groped her boobs. 'Cool, Dad! Can I do that with Jane this weekend?' What am I going to say?"

"Ask your mother," Angie giggled.

"I'll assume if it's your kid, you'll say yes and skip that part," Robert said with a straight face. Angie stuck her tongue out at him and laughed.

"Angie, when our kids are in school, you're going to be the perfect mother who goes to all their school activities and is on a first-name basis with all their teachers, just like my mom is. Maybe all our teachers will be retired by then, and no one will remember who you were."

"You aren't going to your kids' school functions?" Angie asked.

"Of course I will, if I can. What if I'm a famous writer, though? I might be on book tours and not always be able to be there. I'll have to send Robert."

"Write your book first before you declare yourself Felicity Parr," Robert yawned.

"What do you know about Felicity Parr?" I asked.

"Mom and Liz are huge fans. They have all her books. Dad's read most of them, I think. I've read a couple. She's really good."

Angie and I smiled. We couldn't tell him the truth yet.

The first thing I learned about swimming in the pond was how cold it could be. It did warm up as the summer went on, but the creeks that fed and drained the pond cycled the water, and the center of the pond was a good eight feet deep at least. It was never going to pass for bath water, and diving in and getting the shock over with was simply what you did to get used to it.

Robert and Angie were both good swimmers. I wasn't in their league. I knew how to swim, but other than swimming for gym class at school and trips to the city pool, I didn't get nearly as many opportunities to practice as they did. I planned on practicing every day I could over the summer to get better at it so I could be their equal. Hannah had a diving platform anchored over the deepest part of the pond that made a nice resting place and relay point for races. The three of us decided to take a break and sun ourselves there.

"Hey, what's this compartment used for?" Robert asked, pointing to one corner of the platform.

"Emergency supply cabinet," Angie said. "We keep a few necessities in there: suntan lotion, condoms, lube, whiskey…"

"Wait, what? Don't tell me we're lying on your sex pad?" I shouted.

"Relax! You won't get pregnant from lying on the surface!" Angie laughed. "We always clean the tile off after we play, anyway."

"Nobody could see us here, right?" Robert nervously asked.

"Not unless they drove up from the house or flew over us," Angie said. "This is our own little world here. When the time comes, I want to get pregnant here at least once. Maybe that kid will have a better life than I did. I can hope, right?"

"Maybe do it at night so you could wish on a star," Robert pondered. "I don't think Joey would mind."

"That sounds like something you wouldn't mind, Mr. Astronomy Buff!" I gave him a playful nudge. "But I get it. That's what we both want—a better life for our kids than we ever had. I'd want them to grow up here and have this as part of their everyday life. Hell, even in winter, we could bring them out here and ice skate on the pond. I'd love to learn how to do that."

"You'll be the one to inherit it," Angie said. "Your Hannah's only relative she wants anything to do with. More reason to make you my lover, if I get to stay here permanently."

"That's my line!" Robert said. The two of them looked at each other, nodded, and both started kissing me.

"Knock it off, you two! "I giggled. "Convince me I want either of you! That's what this whole dating thing is for."

"You can't write without me, dear! I'm your muse…your demon. I whisper the dark thoughts into your head; you'll make millions off me one day." Angie was proud as a peacock, saying that.

"I think you're cute and funny and fun to hang out with," Robert said. "I dream of you every night."

"Something perverted, I'll bet." I winked at him. I didn't mind at all if he did.

He was still innocent enough to blush. "I'm fourteen. That happens."

"Do you dream of just me, or is Angie there, too?" I grinned at him. I knew the answer, of course. I just wanted him to say it.

"Joey said girl on girl is hot…"

"What has your boyfriend been filling my boyfriend's head with, demon?"

Angie didn't answer in words. She embraced me and started kissing me exactly like we'd practiced. I didn't protest, either. I went along with it, and we put on a show, French kissing each other and playing with each other's breasts through our bikini tops. We didn't show anything. We didn't need to. We just had fun and let Robert watch. After a few minutes, we stopped and looked over at Robert. He was spellbound. His eyes were wide as saucers, and he was sporting a noticeable bulge in his swimsuit that hadn't been there earlier.

Angie smiled at him. "Somebody's excited. Did you want to play, too?"

I could see the wheels spinning in his head. He could not believe he was being asked this question. "Say yes," I said. "If you're going to be our husband, you'll need to get used to this."

Robert nodded nervously. "I'll be gentle, I promise."

"On the first time with Sarah, good. I like it gentle now and then, too. But sometimes we don't want you to be gentle. Sometimes we just want you to pound us into submission and take our breath away. That's something you learn with practice and something you and your partner figure out together."

Robert received his first lesson there on the platform that day. Angie and I took turns French kissing him for half an hour, pausing to kiss each other to give him a chance to catch his breath periodically. No one took their suit off. Our hands stayed above board, but they went everywhere and felt everything. There wasn't any jealousy. At the end, we just curled up together and felt the waves rock us gently on our floating love nest. Three silly teenagers in love with an impossible idea that none of us was prepared to let go, no matter what the world said.

CHAPTER 23

Robert's sister Liz had her own apartment, which she shared with two roommates. She was twenty-three, independent, and didn't need to run home regularly to see everyone. She was happy with her own life and her own place in it. She called her family once a week and came home for holidays and birthdays. Other than that, she was dedicated to her chemistry studies and was all business. That is not to say she was not interested in her brother's first official girlfriend. Quite the opposite! Robert had told her all about me. Because he was transparent as glass, he also told her about Angie. When he did, Liz read him the riot act. When he refused to back down, she called her parents and shouted at them. From what Robert said over the phone later, Brenda had the loudest fight with Liz he'd ever witnessed.

Liz wanted to meet me. She brought Robert to our house one afternoon, and we met in the kitchen, with Mom serving us cookies and milk and inviting them to stay for dinner. Robert accepted. Liz said she'd think about it. These two were not on the same page in life. When Mom left us, Liz gave me a critical stare.

"Why do you like Robert?"

I smiled at him and held his hand. "He's smart and understanding. He's kind. He knows all about music, meadowlarks, turtles, and stars. He describes the universe to me, and I see it through his eyes for the first time. I get excited by it. I want him to show me more—all the things my father and the church tried to hide from me. I want us to go places, do things, and see where life takes us. He respects me as a person, and I feel safe with him. I love him deeply."

"I'm not a romantic," Liz said. "I'll have to take your word on that." She looked at me sternly. "And Angie?"

"Is none of your concern," Robert said sharply. "If it doesn't bother me, it need not concern you."

"Your happiness concerns me. I don't want to see you get hurt because Sarah decides she prefers girls one day and leaves you heartbroken."

"Then that's life," Robert snapped. "I knew this going in. Sarah was honest with me. I think she's worth loving, even if there's a risk involved."

"The risk to Robert is not going to be me leaving him for Angie. The risk is going to come from people like you who are so entrenched in seeing the world one way that they cannot possibly comprehend that others exist in this world! And he's still willing to be there for us! That makes him amazing in my book. You, on the other hand…" Robert put his hand over my mouth so I couldn't finish.

Liz took a bite out of a cookie, sat back in her chair, and stared intently at me. "You dream of being a writer. You have that saucy impertinence that people will call passion if you ever make it big. Apparently, writing has made your aunt a few bucks if she can afford stately Wayne Manor here. Maybe there will be a little magic in your genes to pull it off. For your sake, I hope there is. It's hard raising a family on a teacher's salary. Mom has always carried us with her income. If you don't pull through, my brother must support the two of you."

Liz stayed for dinner. She spent the evening talking about life with Mom and Erin and learning what made our household tick. Liz was nothing like her brother or either of her parents. She was someone who had sacrificed a great deal to achieve success as a student. I wondered if she ever regretted leaving some of those frivolous things behind that made life worth living. That was a topic that I wanted to interview her about one day. Not today, though. Today was just getting her not to hate me.

It was late, and Liz and Robert were getting ready to leave when Angie arrived home from dinner and a movie with Kelcee. She walked into the living room where we were, immediately recognized a stranger was there, and then realized Robert was present. "Sister?"

"Yes," I said.

Liz looked at her with utter disdain. Angie had dealt with reactions like hers throughout her relationship with her partners. She sized her opponent up and stepped over to meet her. "How much older?"

"Nine years," Liz said. "I wanted to meet his girlfriend."

"Which one?" Angie quipped.

"The intelligent one, clearly." Liz wasn't amused.

"Read the room, dear," Erin said. "Go upstairs and let us handle this. You aren't his girlfriend, and you know it."

"Still in school?" Angie asked.

"Studying for my master's in chemistry."

Angie nodded. "You have quite the imposing aura, Liz. I'm not scared by it."

"That's enough! Go upstairs!" Erin growled.

"Stay out of their relationship, if you know what's good for you." Liz hissed.

"You're afraid of me. You should be, too. If I ever kissed you, I'd crack that icy mask you wear in the blink of an eye. You'd beg to be my girlfriend, and I'd do things to you that would make your head explode." With that missile fired, she walked upstairs and left Liz a flustered mess in her wake.

"Do you normally let your daughter act up like that?" Liz asked in frustration.

"My daughter and your brother are my problem and your parents' problem, not yours. I'd suggest you stay out of things if you want to keep peace in your family." My mother was not amused by Liz and let her know it in no uncertain terms. Whatever her level of discomfort with my choice in a relationship, she was going to defend me at all costs.

"I think Liz meant that question for me," Erin replied. "I'll deal with Angie. But I'll give you fair warning, dear—that child of mine has some scary powers. Don't let her kiss you, fondle you, braid your hair, or whisper in your ear if you value your virtue. You're on her radar. She will come for you if you give her the chance. Stay out of her way and don't interfere unless you fancy eating pussy the rest of your life."

Liz's face turned beet red. So did mine. "Why didn't you warn me about the hair braiding?"

Erin smiled and shrugged. "You're smart and adorable. I wouldn't mind it if she kept you around."

It was at this point that Hannah wandered into the room searching for Erin. "Sorry to intrude. I need to borrow you for some managerial advice. They're pushing for a September '96 release on *Belladonna,* but that's too soon. I'm only two-thirds done with the first draft."

"Let me see what they wrote, and I'll figure out what to tell them. Excuse me. Duty calls."

"*Belladonna*?" Liz stared at Hannah in disbelief. If you're writing *Belladonna*, does that make you Felicity Parr?"

Hannah was dumbfounded. "Oh, shit! Who are you?"

"Liz Hill. I'm Robert's older sister. I have all your books. So does my mom!"

"I see! Erin, will you draw up a non-disclosure agreement for her to sign? Obviously, my identity is a secret, and we need to keep it that way."

After some horse trading in Erin's office, Liz took Robert home, along with two freshly autographed Felicity Parr novels and Erin's firm promise to make sure Angie behaved. I wondered if he'd be grounded because of what happened. He was not. Liz never said a word of it to her parents. Mrs. Hill's autographed copy was explained as a late Christmas gift that Liz had misplaced.

***

Kelcee turned up at the house unexpectedly one afternoon and popped in to see Angie briefly. Both of us were surprised to see her, as she usually worked for her mother five days a week during the summer.

"I am working," she said when she found us peeling vegetables out on the patio. "Mom had me run some papers to

185

the courthouse in Jackson. Looks like you're working for Tina today. Sucks to be you."

Angie let out a long sigh. "Tina says this is good experience for when we're housewives.

"Dear God, let me be a success as a writer so I can hire someone to do this!" I laughed.

"Be honest," Kelcee replied. "If you aren't a writer, what are you going to do with yourself? You'll need an extra income if Robert's a teacher. Unless you plan on sponging off your aunt for the rest of your life."

"That's not my style," I replied. "If I couldn't write, I think I would want to either teach or be a guidance counselor. I would want to help people escape from bad situations like I did."

Kelcee nodded. "That fits your character. Hannah would certainly help you with the latter, and Charli would love a protégé she could guide. My dad golfs with her dad a lot. She's very pleased with how kind your mother is. She talks about Tina a lot."

I smiled inwardly. That was good to know!

Kelcee promptly sat down on Angie's lap and kissed her. She then looked over at me. "I hear you've been taking lessons."

I swallowed hard. "Is that a problem?"

"I don't know yet. You aren't allowed to be better in bed than I am."

"Maybe Robert and I should take lessons from you then," I quipped.

The two of them giggled at this suggestion. "Why would you ever want to take lessons from us?" Kelcee asked. "You two could have a wonderful, fulfilling life just being yourselves. You'd be the perfect couple. You know you would."

"But then I wouldn't get to make out with Angie!" I protested. "I like that, too!"

"What did you do to her, you nasty demon?" Kelcee purred at Angie. "You're corrupting her just like you did me. Are you going to make her do what I do?"

"Sarah can choose whatever path she likes. If she wants that, I'll teach her that. If she's happy with less, I'll still fuck her anyway. You chose what you chose. I just helped you become who you wanted to be. I'll do the same for her."

That was not the answer Kelcee expected. "But you like that stuff we do."

Angie kissed her and playfully shoved her hands underneath Kelcee's skirt for a quick feel. "I do. Absolutely, one hundred percent, I love to be that person. What is it you and Joey tell me all the time, though? Sooner or later, I need to grow up. If I stay with you and let Sarah and Robert go off on their own, I want her to be strong and capable. I don't want to ruin her. What kind of friend would that make me if I did that?"

"We study together to make each other better as students and friends," I said quietly. You and Joey helped welcome me in, and I will love you forever for that."

Kelcee got up and straightened her skirt. "You've come a long way since Christmas," she said. "I'm proud of you. Just understand, I was here first. I love Angie, and I don't want to give her up."

"Who said anything about that? You and Angie are still a couple, and I don't want to break you up. I'm happy with Robert. If you do break up, then things might change."

"And if you ever broke up with Robert, things might change, too," she said, kissing me boldly before making her leave to return to work. It occurred to me as I watched her go that I really didn't need to worry about Angie corrupting me. I was doing far too good a job of that myself.

CHAPTER 24

If I was going camping with Robert and his family, I would need some gear. Jerry and Robert decided to take me shopping one afternoon. When they showed up, however, I found Lucy and Brian tagging along. They hadn't seen me since school ended. We wound up buying a tent, a life jacket, extra paddles for canoeing, bug spray, a lantern, cooking utensils, and a lot of other small odds and ends. The Hills were taking me camping in Onaway State Park in the northern part of Michigan's Lower Peninsula. I had never been outside Southeastern Michigan except for a class trip to the state capital in Lansing in fifth grade. I had no idea what awaited me up there. Would there be bears? Mr. Hill didn't seem to think that was likely. Pity. I might want to see a real bear.

We ate lunch at the mall and then drove home. Mr. Hill had other things to do in the afternoon, so he dropped us all off with the idea he'd come back later and pick everyone up. What neither he nor Brian's nor Lucy's parents knew was that Hannah was in Detroit meeting with her publisher. Erin, as her business manager, was also there, and she'd dragged Angie along to observe. Mom was busy writing and really didn't want to be bothered with chaperoning us. Therefore, it came down to me asking Mom if we could go out to the pond to do sketch work.

"No problem," she said. "Take the truck and don't drive it into the lake. Jerry is supposed to pick them up around four, so be back here by then."

"Not a problem," I said, hugging her.

With that, we set off to the barn and got in the truck. I'd watched Angie drive it, so I had an idea how it worked. Hannah or Erin must have taken the truck out at some point because the seat was set for someone at least half a foot taller than I was. Robert had to adjust it for me. I didn't drive fast, but I drove safely. We all arrived at the pond, piled out, and got to work sketching after getting our suntan lotion applied. Lucy had Brian posing on the dock with a fishing pole in his hand. I had Robert pose in the pickup truck's bed. We drew for about ninety minutes. By then, we had most of the basic outlining and shading done and could finish the rest on our own time. We let our models loose, and we decided to go swimming.

"What are the odds your mother would come up here?" Lucy asked

"Not impossible, but I'd say highly unlikely. Why do you ask? Fancy going skinny dipping or something?"

She laughed. "I wish! I would love to do it sometime, but I'm not ready to do it with the guys here."

I nodded. "I'm not ready yet, either."

"I thought you two had seen each other naked," Robert asked Brian.

"When we were younger. Now that we're dating, she's gotten shy."

"It's different now!" Lucy said. "Mom watches you and me like a hawk now. So do your parents."

"I don't think it's a big deal," Brian yawned. "You've got your parts, and I've got mine. Just because we see them doesn't mean we need to start making babies."

"I don't see you getting naked," Lucy shot back.

Brian gave Robert a friendly nudge. "I will if you will."

The reality of the situation dawned on all of us. We could absolutely do it, and no one would be the wiser. The question was, would anyone be brave enough to?

"As much as we want to see your dicks, it's not going to happen today," I said firmly. "Lucy said no, and I'm good with that. If she changes her mind, she'll let us know. You need to move at her pace, Brian. Don't be weird."

"Sorry," Brian said. "It just sounded like fun."

"It will be," Lucy smiled. "You think I don't want to jump your bones right now? Part of me does, but I want to wait until I'm at least sixteen for sure. I'm not Angie and Kelcee. I'm not in a hurry to give it up the first chance I'm alone with you."

Brian understood that. The two of them had been friends for so long that they cared deeply for one another, even if they loved getting on each other's nerves. The two of them hugged. Lucy ducked into the changing room and popped out wearing a cute green bikini. Brian went next, and the two of them headed out onto the pond to swim. Robert and I hung back.

"They're sorting things out," I said. "I don't think their path is going as smoothly as ours is." Robert was lost in thought, with a strange grin on his face. "What perverted thing are you pondering, Mr. Hill?" I asked him.

He was embarrassed that I'd caught him out. "Just doing some calculations in my head. Two people could fit in that changing booth."

"Are you serious? You want us to change together?"

"I know, it's not going to happen. But it was fun thinking about it."

It was fun—too much fun. I smiled. "Let's do it. We can strip out of our clothes and put our suits on in sixty seconds, right?"

All it took was one stupid grin from him. We grabbed our swimsuits, ran for the changing room, and frantically changed while trying not to get tangled up with each other. We glimpsed each other naked in the process, but that wasn't our priority. This wasn't romantic. This wasn't overtly sexual. This was a tease, and we loved it. Once we were in our suits, we ran out of the cabana and put our clothes on the picnic table in separate piles. We then ran for the dock and dived into the water.

"What were you two perverts doing?" Lucy squealed.

"Hey, you said we had to wear suits," Robert reminded her. "That's exactly what we're doing."

"We just decided we wanted a quick flash," I giggled. "Now that we scratched that itch, we can relax and have fun."

We swam for an hour and had a great time. Lucy and Brian had a quiet chat and then asked if they could have some alone time together. They went back to shore, spread out some beach towels, and curled up together having a kissing session. Robert and I decided to swim out to the diving platform and rest there to give them all the privacy they needed.

"I didn't give you all that you wanted, but did you like what you saw?" I laughed.

He leaned over and kissed me. "I'll be dreaming of it for a long time."

I gazed up at the sky and watched a hawk lazily circling above us. "Having Brian and Lucy here made it easier. There's no pressure for us to do anything. We can just enjoy the pond and enjoy ourselves."

"But we want it, right?"

"Of course, silly! For the time being, we're stuck teasing each other, but it felt good."

"Like that's a bad thing," Robert said. "The more comfortable we get with each other, the less stressful it will be when the time comes."

"My father would kill me if he knew what I was doing right now," I said. "Then again, in the world I grew up in, Jesus could see everything you did from Heaven, so I'm probably already on my way to Hell. You'll follow me, won't you?"

Robert smiled mischievously. "Or you'll follow me."

"Because I love you or something?"

"Because I am amazing!" he said. He stood up and stuck his tongue out at me. "I am the Lord and Master of this Pond! Bow before me!"

Dear God, that sent me into hysterics! He acted the role of a total megalomaniac perfectly. Sadly, his lordship's reign was brief. I shoved him in the water and dived in after him. We swam a bit more, crawled back onto the platform, and sprawled out.

"Must be getting close to three o'clock," Robert said. We'll have to start back to shore soon."

"I kind of like you being a little more dominant," I said. "Stay that way."

"Liz told me I had better learn to stand up for myself if I'm going to handle you."

We lay there floating in the middle of the lake, holding hands and trading kisses until it was time to swim back. Brian and Lucy had already gotten dressed, and they flipped us a pair of towels to dry off with. We walked over and grabbed our clothes.

"Want to do it again?" Robert playfully asked.

"Yes, but different this time." We walked into the cabana together. I didn't think twice. I just stripped off my suit.

"Do you mind? I may not see you like this for a while. I'd like to enjoy it a little while longer."

"Will that help?"

He nodded. "You are so fucking beautiful."

I picked up my bra and handed it to him. He put it on me with a little coaching and encouragement. We proceeded to dress each other in that cramped space, savoring the touch and feel of our most intimate places but not making anything overtly sexual out of it. This was practice for the future. With some luck, we'd be doing this for each other for decades to come.

Lucy and Brian were curious. We explained what we'd done. Somehow, the weirdness of it struck a chord in Lucy, who told Brian she'd make him practice putting a bra on her someday. Brian giggled at the idea, and they happily kissed as we loaded the truck to return to the house. Fortunately, we arrived about ten minutes before Mr. Hill did. Seeing me driving might have gotten him a little out of shape. We showed off our sketches to Mom and Jerry, gave each other hugs, and exchanged furtive smiles behind the adults' backs.

After everyone had left, Mom pulled me aside. "How was your first time behind the wheel?"

"A little nerve-wracking, but fun. I'm not ready for the road yet."

"Good." She paused. "Anything else you want to tell me?"

I took a deep breath. "I'm still a virgin. I won't make it until I'm married, though. Not even close."

Mom sighed deeply and nodded. "I can't say I'm surprised. You two seem like you're in a big hurry to grow up. Do we need to get you on the pill?"

"Not yet. Not this summer. We're not even close to being ready for that yet. I promise I'll tell you if I change my mind."

"Thanks," she said, hugging me tightly. "Is he worth it?"

"Worth what? Losing my virginity over? What the hell did that do for you? Dad took yours on your wedding night, and it didn't make you any happier in the end. Yes, Robert is worth it. I want to be with him for the rest of my life. You know he's better than Dad. You shouldn't even have to ask me that question."

"He is better than Daniel," Mom sighed. "You know how much it hurts me to say that? I should be here lecturing you about how irresponsible you are at your age--how you need to wait for the right person to come along so you'll have a good life and become a godly woman worthy of respect."

I smiled. "Isn't that what you are doing?"

"I played by the rules. I was good. I tried everything I knew to be a good wife, mother, and woman. I got nothing for it but abuse and hatred. How do I lecture you when Robert would move heaven and earth to make you happy? He's fourteen going on fifteen and more of a man than your father ever was or will be in his entire miserable life. My marriage is over. I'm writing and throwing my feelings on paper. I'm having fantasies about Charli, and I don't know what to do. I am the most depraved of sinners…and I'm happy now. I'm finally happy. How do I lecture you? I don't know!"

She was crying when she spoke those words. I thought they might be happy tears. I wasn't sure. "Trust me when I say this. If you decide you want to ask Charli, I think she'll give you a chance. I just get the feeling you're both searching for something in life, and maybe that's each other."

"So, what did you and Robert do? Be honest."

"I taught him how to put my bra on."

Mom was incredulous. "You had the whole pond to yourself, and that's what you accomplished?"

"We're not ready for sex yet, Mom. We like what we see of each other. When it's time, we'll take the next step forward. But it isn't time yet. For the moment, we're just happy to be together and have fun. That's what being a teenager is all about."

"I seem to remember it being about getting Cokes at the mall and mission trips to California when I was your age. Times have changed a lot. Having a boy put my bra on was never something I could imagine doing. I wouldn't have asked your father to do it, either. That's just not something women do."

"Bet you and Charli will get good dressing and undressing each other," I grinned and hugged her.

"Don't put ideas in my head!" She hugged me back, though I did get a couple of swats on my rump for misbehaving. Nothing like the kind Dad gave me. More like the kind I'd expect from Angie.

We are mother and daughter. We've been together our whole lives. It is awkward now because we have changed so much in so little time. At times, we don't recognize each other, and we struggle to recognize ourselves in the mirror. It's a strange kind of afterlife. Our previous selves have died, and there's no bringing them back. We've tasted the fruit and now know what was kept from us all these years. It has a bittersweet flavor, this knowledge. It comes with uncertainty and doubt. It comes with confusion. All the answers aren't in a book to tell us how to live, though Mom is still trying hard to pretend they are. We just struggle through day to day and work it out ourselves. We must find our own meaning in the chaos that is life. Gods, we are not. We're ephemeral mortals drawn to the flame of life like so many moths. Life is beautiful. Life sometimes burns us. All things considered, I'd still rather fly.

CHAPTER 25

Camping was an experience. After my first time, I confess I am not completely sold on the idea. I like my bed. Sleeping in a tent was nowhere near as comfortable. Camp toilets were disgusting. Jerry telling jokes around the campfire killed my brain cells slowly and painfully. Those things leave so much to be desired! On the positive side, I found I really loved being outside and experiencing the wind and water. I loved swimming. Robert taught me how to canoe, and we spent time every non-rainy day out on the water just talking about life as we paddled. Robert loved to fish, and I learned how to bait a hook. Not my favorite thing in the world, but it allowed me to spend time with my guy, and I was willing to overlook the worm's sad demise for that privilege.

Bless his heart, Robert's the perfect significant other for a writer. He listened to my ideas, offered his input, which was often very useful, and remembered things that I had forgotten. He left me alone when I needed time to write. He had his own interests and didn't need me to entertain him. If I needed him just to be there and keep me company, he'd curl up next to me. We took a nap together every afternoon in his tent. Jerry and Brenda didn't seem to mind, and I always woke up inspired to write more. He recharged my batteries somehow. I don't understand how it worked, but I am grateful for it.

We were in the country, away from the lights of the city. The stars were more numerous and beautiful than I'd ever seen them, living in the city my whole life. Jerry and Robert gave me an astronomy lesson, pointing out the planets and constellations. Robert brought a telescope along, and on clear nights, we got to see the moons of Jupiter, the rings of Saturn, and the craters of our own Moon. For the Hill family, all of this was normal. For me, this was a revelation. I saw it as a small introduction to the amazing universe we called home.

Saturday was our last night camping together, though I think we all decided we wanted to do it again next year. We sang around the campfire. We talked about the things we enjoyed and the things we learned from our time together. For me, it was about exploring our physical limits, doing things we'd never done. I had been a very sedentary creature for most of my life. Getting rousted out of that lifestyle to swim, hike, and canoe gave me sore muscles but allowed me to challenge my limits. Jerry and Brenda learned more about me and solidified the bond we shared.

When Robert's turn came, he just smiled at me. "I just fell in love more," he said.

"You'd say that if you took her to McDonald's. Isn't there something more concrete you'd like to tell us?"

"I think Sarah would rather be home writing than out here with us. She's so full of ideas right now, and we're keeping her from working on them full-time. But she's here, dealing with mosquitoes and rain and mud and pit toilets because she cares about us so much and because she wants to explore our world. She's curious about so many things, and I love sharing the moments with her as she discovers them."

I smiled inwardly. I knew what I wanted to do that night. When it came time for bed, I told Brenda I was sharing Robert's tent for the last night. She gave me a kind but stern look. "No messing around. Just sleeping."

"I am not going to do anything that will get me pregnant. I want to cuddle with him."

I told Robert I was sleeping with him, and I brought my pillow over from my tent. He made room for me, and I snuggled up in his sleeping bag with him. "We're being good until everyone goes to bed," I said. "Then I'm getting comfortable and so are you."

He gave me a cheesy grin. "I think my folks are probably doing that tonight, too. They always have sex on the last night of camp. It's a family tradition. They try to hide that they do it, but Liz and I always knew."

We waited for everyone else to fall asleep. When all was quiet and we felt safe, I slid out of his sleeping bag and stripped down to my underwear. Robert did the same. Then we crawled back in the bag and snuggled up together. I kissed him. "This is ridiculous. Your parents are out there."

He smiled sheepishly. "Yes, they are."

"And they know we're in here. We told them."

"Don't do anything stupid!" Robert laughed, imitating his father's voice. "And we won't."

"Who has parents who think this sort of thing is okay? We should be on one of those weird talk shows with people who marry their uncles."

Robert grinned at me. "If I end up in a relationship with you and Angie, we probably will be."

I lay back on my pillow and sighed. "I'm doomed."

"Nah," he replied and kissed me. "My parents hated being dismissed and disrespected when they were in love at our age. They want us to have the respect they never received. They'll give us this freedom if we behave responsibly."

I lay beside him and thought about Mom. "I can't imagine my mother wanting this when she was my age. Our families are all about modesty, decorum, and Jesus. Except for Hannah. No one can explain Hannah."

"Or you," Robert chuckled. "Two peas in a pod, you are."

I felt safe beside him. We drifted off to sleep in each other's arms. After a couple of hours, we woke up to muffled grunting and moaning. Robert's parents were obviously having sex, and the two of us started giggling at the thought of it.

"No sleeping until they're finished," I whispered. "Do you want to make out?"

"May as well," he grinned.

It took Jerry and Brenda twenty minutes to conclude their business—twenty minutes we spent happily French kissing and playfully groping inside a sleeping bag. It was too dark to see much of each other in the tent, so we relied on our hands to feel the parts of our bodies we had first seen at the pond. We were trying our hardest to be quiet, but sometimes that wasn't possible because we'd start laughing. I loved this boy more than anything else in the world. Right then, I was the happiest I'd ever been in life, and at that moment, it seemed a good idea to crawl on top of Robert and sit on him.

"If you're lord of the pond, I'm queen of the tent."

He suddenly sat up, and I had to hook my legs around him to keep my balance. Something very hard was twitching beneath me. "I'm king of the bag, baby," he whispered.

"That is so fucking corny. Did you learn that from your dad?" I kissed him, and we wrestled playfully. The rest of our clothes were soon discarded, and we realized we had to break this off before we went too far. We were both breathing heavily.

"C-c-can I ask you a question?" Robert stammered.

I grinned at him. "You already are. What is it?"

He took a deep breath. "I know I'm early and all, and I know we have Angie to deal with. I just know I want to be with you for the rest of my life. Wanna get married someday?"

"Mmhmmm," I replied as I softly kissed him.

We curled up in the sleeping bag and spent the rest of the night cuddled together. When morning came, we dressed each other and left the tent to get the fire started and make breakfast. Eventually, Jerry and Brenda appeared, looking happy but very tired. Jerry started boiling water for coffee.

"Slept well, I hope?" Brenda asked.

Robert hugged her. "Very well," he said. Lying to his mother so brazenly! "Feels nice to have someone beside you. I could get used to that."

Brenda laughed. "You've got a few years before that happens," she said. "I'm also your mother, and you will have to do a lot better trying to pull the wool over my eyes than that. We woke you up, didn't we?"

I nodded. "For a little while, yes."

"Sorry about that. Grownups still get horny now and then, too. You'll learn that when you get to be our age, and your kids roll their eyes at you."

"It didn't last long," Robert said. "We just made out for a while until you finished."

"Then we went back to sleep," I hastily added. "Still virgins."

"Thank you for that," Jerry mumbled as he wandered over. He stared at Robert and shook his head. "Anyone ever tell you that you share too much stuff I don't want to hear?"

"I intend to have that conversation with him later," I said, playfully stomping on Robert's foot to emphasize the point.

"You get mad at Liz for not sharing enough," his wife said in a calm but forceful tone. "He wants us to know he's being careful, and I appreciate that. Just remember, it's okay to keep some secrets to yourself. We don't need to know everything. We trust you to do the right thing."

"Don't disappoint us," Jerry added, smiling warmly at me. "I am not going to mind one bit if I watch you marry my son in a few years. If you're going to fall in love young, pick a good man who will stand by you for life."

I took Robert by the hand and embraced him. "I think I already have."

***

When I got home, I found the situation around the mansion had shifted temporarily. Hannah had been called upon to provide emergency housing for a young mother with two children until safe passage could be arranged to get her home to Arizona. Our wing of the house was suddenly more cramped and noisier. The children were aged three and one. The mother could only speak broken English, but Angie knew some Spanish from school, and Mom knew a few words. Angie was a natural with kids. I didn't hesitate, either. This was where I got to pay the universe back for my good fortune in being rescued. This is where I got to do God's work, even if I wasn't sure any god was there to see my deeds. If there weren't, it still filled my heart with joy to make a difference, even if those children would never remember me when they grew older.

Mom asked Angie where she had learned how to raise children. "Here," she said proudly. "I remember my mom trying to look after me, but she had it hard. All these mothers do."

"I will never put myself in a position of needing to be rescued again," I said. "I would choose to be by myself for the rest of my life before I give up my personal rights to any partner."

CHAPTER 26

The first meeting of the summer study club was called to order the week after my camping trip. It felt good to see everyone in person again, though I had talked to everyone on the phone at least once since school let out. Everyone in our group was present except for Joey, Kelcee, and Chad. Joey and Kelcee were working, of course. Chad was away at a basketball camp. Melanie and Yuki were in charge. They had our entire day planned out: two hours of study, one hour in the weight room, an hour-long lunch break, two more hours of study, and then the rest of the afternoon at the pond. Kelcee had prepared specialized homework assignments for each of us to complete based on our projected classes for the coming semester. We sat down and cracked open our books, but we were all talking as we were working. The atmosphere was very informal. Our study sessions always were.

Angie was with us. As she was a senior and we were all sophomores, her work was completely different from ours. "Why are you even here?" Lucy asked. "It's not like we could help you figure out your homework."

"Kelcee said to figure out everything I know today so she knows what to help me with next time we see each other," Angie replied. "Plus, there are so many smart people in this room, somebody probably would know the answer anyway, even if we aren't in the same grade."

"Makes sense," Dee said. "Plus, you get to hang out with Sarah and Robert." She winked at Angie, and Angie smiled back.

"Behave yourselves," Yuki growled. "I'm watching you!" Robert stuck his tongue out at her.

"You survived your camping trip, I see," Melanie said. "Going to do it again next year?"

"Yes," I said with a broad smile on my face. "I had a great time."

"You must really love Robert if you put up with Mr. Hill in the wild for a week," Dan laughed.

"Nothing like listening to him sing 'Oh! Susanna,' while casting for fish at seven in the morning," I smiled.

Yuki shook her head. "How does he expect to catch any fish doing that? You must be quiet like a ninja while you fish, otherwise you'll scare them away. My father fishes on weekends. He will outcatch Mr. Hill every time."

"Do you fish?" Robert asked.

"I do. I'll catch more fish than you any day. I was taught by a master," Yuki said proudly.

"Bring your gear next time. We'll have a competition. Loser sings 'Oh! Susanna' in their underwear on the dock," Lucy cackled.

"I am not singing anything in my underwear, thank you very much!" Yuki snapped.

"So, you plan on losing then? Guess that means I'm better at fishing," Robert said triumphantly. "I am lord and master of the pond, after all."

"Until I threw your dumb ass in the water!" I giggled.

"Would you do it in front of everyone?" Yuki asked sarcastically.

"Hell, yes," Robert paused in thought, "I'd sing it naked if I had to. But I won't have to, because I'm better."

This entire exchange was getting under Yuki's skin, and everyone knew it. Yuki was an overachiever who hated losing, and she definitely was better at fishing than Robert.

"Like you'd really do it," she said defensively.

"One way to find out: take the bet. Or are you…chicken?" Lucy flapped her arms and clucked after she spoke. Yuki threw a pencil at her.

I looked over at Robert. "I'm curious now. Tell you what, Yuki. If you lose, I'll sing it for you. Now you don't have an excuse not to take the bet."

Yuki stared at Robert. "Your girlfriend's honor will remain intact because I will not lose. Game on. Next study session."

"Deal!" The two shook hands, and we were going to have a fishing competition.

***

For me, July 4, 1995, was a big deal. It was my first Independence Day as a Powell, no longer under the dominion of my father and the Brenner clan. Liberation was very real and very meaningful. Mom and I were very reflective on all that had happened. The fireworks were more impressive in Detroit or Ann Arbor than they were in South Lyon. The main attraction of watching them locally was not having to drive into the city,

209

fight traffic, or deal with the sheer number of people those bigger cities drew. We could just as easily eat hot dogs and hamburgers, listen to bands play, and watch the fireworks closer to home, then rush home and light sparklers and firecrackers. Spending time with our family and friends was more important than anything else. This year, the family aspect would be a bit different. I would be going with Jerry, Brenda, Robert, and Liz. Mom was coming along, too, but to our pleasant surprise, Charli had agreed to join our group. I was amazed Mom asked her. I knew she wanted to, but making the leap of faith to call and ask was a sign Mom was coming to terms with her feelings. There wasn't anything romantic attached to it yet. They were just hanging out as friends. That's all they needed to do right now, and it was going to happen. I was thrilled for her.

Angie was going, but she would be with Joey and Kelcee. She told me up front that I probably wouldn't see her. I understood. This was their time, and the sands of that hourglass were quickly running out. Angie was grateful that I wasn't angry or possessive. We had a long, heartfelt kiss before she left the house. It was her way of reassuring me she still loved me.

The fireworks were beautiful that night. Robert and I held hands and cuddled together. It was the conversation going on beside me that was more interesting. Mom and Charli had been engaging in small talk all evening, but things became more interesting as the fireworks began.

"Tina, do you think you'll ever get married again?" Charli asked.

Mom shook her head. "No. I know not all men are like Daniel, but I just don't feel like that kind of relationship is something I want anymore. Sarah's having better luck than I am. She can be the Powell woman who gets married next." She glanced at Charli. "What about you? I've never heard you discuss guys."

"You won't, either. I'm a lesbian. Is that going to be a problem?"

"A year ago, it would have. Not now." A large boom echoed through the skies as a brilliant bunch of fireworks exploded over our heads. "I wonder if maybe that's the direction I'm heading," Mom said quietly. "I'm not sure yet. I'm feeling things I've never dealt with before, and it scares me a little."

Charli smiled at her. "I remember what it was like when I was Sarah's age, trying to make sense of those feelings. It was hard for me then. I can imagine how hard it is for you now." She put her hand on top of my mother's. "If you need someone to talk to, I'm all ears. You're a good friend, and I want to help in any way I can."

"That would mean a lot to me," Mom said, grasping Charli's hand. She then quickly let go. "I should have asked if you were seeing someone. I don't know that I've ever asked!"

Charli's hand found its way back to my mother's. "No, I'm not seeing anyone. I haven't dated much since college." She paused. "Are you...interested in me?"

Mom took a deep breath and exhaled slowly. "I dream of you sometimes. If I decided I wanted to date a woman, I would ask you first. I just haven't quite gotten the courage to make that leap."

Charli squeezed Mom's hand. "If you do, I hope you ask me. I've never dated anyone older than me, so that would be an adjustment I'd have to make. I'd be game to try, if it were you. I hope that doesn't put undue pressure on you."

Mom laughed. "It probably makes the decision easier."

The next voice I heard came from someone I hadn't expected to say anything. "There's nothing quite as nice as watching the fireworks with your arm around someone you love," Jerry said. "It's dark. Nobody's going to notice if the two of you try it and see if it suits you. Just saying." He and Brenda were happily nestling together, just as we were.

"You're a meddler, Jerry!" Mom laughed.

"Want to?" Charli asked, squeezing her hand even tighter.

Mom let go of Charli's hand and gingerly put her arm around her waist. The two of them wordlessly watched the rest of the fireworks that way. When the show ended, they remained in that position, reluctant to give it up right away. Mom had a contented smile on her face, and Charli was looking at her, grinning stupidly.

"That's what love feels like, Mom. I think it suits you."

"Would it be out of line to ask if you wanted to come back to our place and talk?" Mom said nervously.

"I think you should sleep on it tonight and call me tomorrow. If you still want to talk, let me know. I will be there. I've just done things in the moment that haven't worked out well the morning after. I don't want us to lose a friendship because we rushed this."

"Understood. I'll call you tomorrow and let you know how I feel."

Mom did make that call, and the two of them went out for dinner. When she got home, I asked her how it went.

"We are going to take it slow and easy," Mom said, hugging me. "But we think something's there we want to explore. It will take a while. I've got a lot of baggage to work through and so does she—more than you know and stuff I won't tell you."

I hugged her. "No worries. I'm glad there's a spark you two want to nurture. I hope it works out for you."

"Me, too. We compared notes. It seems a couple of people I know have been matchmaking behind the scenes."

"That meddling Mr. Hill!" I laughed.

"Liar! You and Hannah told Charli I might ask her!" She hugged me. "Thank you for that."

"I want to see you both happy. Now you just call her when you're ready to date."

"I'm not at that point yet. We aren't dating. We're hanging out."

"Hanging out is good," I smiled.

"You should try it," Mom said. "You're in way too much of a hurry to be an adult. If I know you, you probably slept in Robert's tent while you were camping."

The difference between Robert and me? I never answered that question. Mom chose not to make me, for which I was eternally grateful.

CHAPTER 27

The rest of the summer was spent primarily on writing my book. Some days, I spent twelve hours or more in my room composing, revising, pondering...or when those options failed, swearing. I learned how to become a writer that summer, with Hannah and Charli reading my work at regular intervals and critiquing it as we went along. At times, the process was contentious. I knew what I wanted to do in my head, and it frustrated me that I couldn't convey it to them. They knew how my work needed to be and struggled to explain why I couldn't do it the way I wanted. One day, my frustration bubbled over, and I just couldn't stand it any longer.

"I know how this needs to be!" I shouted.

"You can't set your story up that way, and you know it," Charli countered.

"Then you write your own mother-fucking story and let me handle mine!" As soon as those words left my mouth, I realized I'd just cursed out my English teacher to her face! "Oh, shit! I am so sorry!"

Hannah chuckled. "Charli, this is what happens every time I write a book. My editor and I fight and call each other every swear word we can think of. Don't take it personally, and feel free to tell my idiot niece to learn some fucking manners or you'll tell her mother she needs to beat the ever-loving shit out of her!"

"You are never going to be able to be in my class again. I can see that right now. Once you get used to cussing me out, you'll just do it out of habit, and I can't have your classmates doing what you do."

"That and the fact you might be dating Mom."

Charli blushed a bit. "Yeah, that's another reason." She turned to Hannah for confirmation. "I can really tell her to listen to her fucking elders once in a while?"

"Absolutely, dear. I never did when I was her age. Look how I turned out!"

It suddenly dawned on me that I didn't know if Charli knew who Hannah was. "Hannah, did you tell her what else you do for a living?"

The two of them exchanged glances and smiled. "I know," Charli said. "Quite the thing to have such a famous aunt! She knows a lot about writing, and I learned a lot from her when I was her student. So, when we tell you to do something, lose the fucking attitude and pay attention!" She glanced over at Hannah. "Like that, huh?"

"Perfect."

For me, the sad thing about this exchange was that it gave me time to further ponder what I'd written that had made them correct me in the first place. They were right. I was wrong. Once I had a chance to examine the issue soberly, I could see it plain as day. "I'll let you win this round," I said. "But next time might be different."

"Next time, is next time," Hannah said. "Fight that battle when you need to."

"You aren't going to tell Mom, are you?"

"That depends on how the rest of the day goes." We went back to work and managed to get through the rest of the session without any other major battles.

***

I woke up hungry about one in the morning and went off to the kitchen in search of some leftover cake. By now, I was used to navigating my way through the mansion in the dark. Seeing a figure in the shadows didn't scare me. I could tell it was Angie right away. It seemed Angie was also suffering from late-night munchies. She smiled at me and cut me a piece of cake. We sat down at the table and began eating. Neither of us spoke at first. I got up and went to the refrigerator to get something to drink. There was a half-filled bottle of Moscato wine that I thought Angie would probably like, so I grabbed it. I set it down on the table and grabbed two wine glasses from the cupboard.

Angie raised her eyebrows slightly. "Two?"

"You won't say anything if I have a little, right?"

Angie smiled. "Of course not. I filled my glass half full and handed the bottle to Angie. Angie filled hers to the top. "Thank you," she said. "It's officially Saturday now. May as well make a night of it."

I took a sip of my wine. "It's sweet!" I giggled. "I like this better than champagne."

"Don't drink too much! I don't want to have to carry you back to your room."

217

"I promise," I said. We ate our cake and drank our wine together in the dark. I felt her foot brushing playfully against my thigh.

Angie smiled. "Care to play a game?"

"I'm not sure. I was just planning on sneaking some cake out of the refrigerator. I didn't plan on meeting you."

Angie reached over and ruffled my hair. "You always want to have a seduction in your mind in case of emergency," she said. "If nothing else, you have something to fantasize about in the middle of class when you're bored. Though you like school, so you probably wouldn't need to think of things like that…"

"If you fantasized less, you might get better grades." I finished my cake. There was a bit of frosting on the side of the plate. I scooped it up with my finger and ran it across my lips. "Kiss me," I said.

I thought it was clever. She snickered a little. "I will. I'm finishing my cake first, though." I sat in my chair with frosting smeared on my lips, feeling stupid for two minutes, and watched her eat. She's playing with me.

I got up, walked over to the patio door, and stared out into the darkness. The sky was clear, and the stars were beautiful. Robert would love to be exploring with his telescope tonight. Angie walked over and embraced me from behind.

"Two shadows in the moonlight," she whispered. "One with messy lips."

"Grab the kitchen timer, will you?" I asked. She handed it to me, and I wound it to exactly five minutes. "You can do anything you want to me before the bell rings."

She understood. We began to kiss furiously in the moonlight. She licked the frosting off my lips and slid her tongue across mine, sharing the taste with me. I felt her fingers unbuttoning my pajama top and her hands cupping my breasts and playing with them. She kissed her way down my neck to my chest and sucked playfully on my nipples. In the background, the ticking continued. How many more seconds were left? I'd lost count in the haze my brain had fallen into. I felt excited. I felt amazing. Her kisses returned to my lips in a feverish fury. She was devouring me, and I was savoring every moment.

Then I felt her hand sliding down my chest and underneath the hem of my pajama shorts. My eyes suddenly widened. Anything in five minutes? She'd taken me at my word. The ticking kept going. She found her target. Oh, fuck! I let out a moan. I had let Robert fumble around down there briefly. Angie was a different matter. She knew exactly what she needed to do to turn me on, and she did it with precision. I had the biggest orgasm of my life, and I was terrified I must have awakened the whole house.

The timer dinged.

Angie's hand pulled out of my shorts. She licked her fingers lasciviously and then kissed me. "How do you feel?"

"Why didn't you throw that thing out the door?" I sighed. "I'd have let you keep going."

"I know you would have," Angie said quietly. "But you aren't ready yet. You and I know it."

"Didn't stop you from putting your hand down my pants."

"Damn right it didn't." She hugged me tightly. "You have no idea how badly I want you right now."

I shook my head. "I think I do. I think I do." I kissed her gently and ran my hands over her T-shirt, feeling her breasts cautiously. "I want to finish this someday."

"We will," she said. "That's a promise."

The shadows slipped away from each other in the night, happy and yet unsatisfied.

CHAPTER 28

The day of the great fishing competition came. Because it was part of our study group, we had to study first. Everyone struggled through the homework, knowing that it was the last thing we really wanted to do. We packed our lunches, took them out to the pond, and ate at the picnic table while Robert and Yuki battled on the dock. The rules were simple. The two of them had one hour to catch as many fish as they could. If they were tied at the end of the hour, there would be no punishment. If Robert lost, he'd have to sing something on the dock in his underwear. If Yuki lost, I would take her punishment. Also, as the fish were not to blame for the contest being held, any fish caught would be immediately released.

Yuki quickly caught a fish. Robert caught one five minutes later. Fifteen minutes passed before Yuki caught another fish. Ten minutes after that, Robert scored again. Then the fish decided they weren't going to play anymore, and the dock grew quiet. Fifty-nine minutes had passed. The score was two fish each. We all started counting down the seconds.

"Guess we tied," Yuki said. "Nobody has to sing."

"I'm okay with that. This was fun." Robert reached over and shook Yuki's hand. "We should go fishing again sometime."

20, 19, 18, 17…

"I'd like that. No bets, though."

12, 11, 10…

"Agreed."

6, 5, 4…and Robert's line suddenly jerked. He quickly started reeling the line in and found he'd caught the smallest, saddest-looking fish in the whole pond. But it was a fish, and Robert won.

"Time ran out!" Yuki yelled.

"The line jerked at three seconds. That's when he caught it," Chad said. We'd made him the official judge of the match since he didn't have any rooting interest in the matter.

Yuki started swearing up an absolute storm in some unknown tongue. I walked out onto the dock and kissed Robert. "Time for your prize, dear." I promptly took off my shoes, pulled off my shirt, unzipped my jeans, and dropped them onto the dock. There I was in front of everyone in my underwear. All I had to do now was sing.

Yuki walked over beside me. "I am so going to regret this." With that, she stripped down to her underwear while our friends looked on in disbelief. Robert decided he'd strip down too, and the Brenner Pond Strippers Trio sang a boisterous rendition of "Oh, Susannah" accompanied by the quacking of the pond's ducks, who found our melody disturbing and voiced their vociferous displeasure. Our friends cheered us loudly. Robert and I shared a hug and kiss.

"You want a hug?" Robert winked at Yuki.

"Not the way you're dressed. You'll probably poke me with something." She smiled, though. We'd chosen to share her punishment, and that meant something to her.

The two of us dived in the water and began swimming. Everyone else changed into their suits and joined us. We had to make a quick stop on the diving platform to throw on sunblock. Melanie popped on for a moment and tapped Robert on the chest.

"Thank God you two wore blue. It would be a bitch if you were showing through right now," she laughed.

"But we would enjoy that!" I said.

"Entirely too much," Melanie laughed. "If I don't go ask Dan something, I'm going to stay on this platform and do something foolish," she said to herself.

"What's that supposed to mean?" Robert asked.

She smiled at him. "I think maybe I want to get a boyfriend of my own. I wish I'd known you'd turn out to be cool when you got older. Guess I'm stuck asking Dan out now."

"Dan is way cuter than I am!" Robert protested.

"Go get him, Melanie!" I shouted.

Melanie dived off the platform and swam over to where Dan was talking with Chad and Dee. Words were exchanged, Dan immediately hugged Melanie, and we knew she'd gotten the answer she wanted.

"I guess she's never going to ask me now," Robert grinned. "Still, that was fun to hear."

"I shall have to soothe your broken heart later, after everyone goes home. Unless you want to cop a feel underwater?"

"That'll work," he grinned. And with that, the great fishing competition came to an end.

****

Joey decided to leave for college during the second week of August. That gave him a month with Kelcee and Angie to wrap things up and decide what they wanted to do. Angie apologized to me up front about the situation.

"I have a month with him. I owe him that, and I'm not going to let things end without doing my best to remind him what he's leaving behind. I'll catch up with you later. I promise. Work on your relationship with Robert while I'm away."

This was overly dramatic. She still lived here, after all, and I saw her pretty much every day. She also had the only bed big enough to fit all three of them comfortably, so they spent most of their last weekends together at the mansion. Mom begrudgingly put up with their presence at breakfast.

Joey made her visibly uneasy. He was eighteen, and I was fifteen. The last thing she was going to allow was any questionable physical contact between us. Joey promised he wouldn't. Kelcee and Angie insisted they wouldn't allow him to do it. Whenever he showed up for breakfast, he'd always smile and greet me the same way.

"Good morning, squirt!"

I smiled back. "May my mother poison your eggs and spit in your coffee." We really did like each other as friends. Depending on which route my life ultimately took, I might even be with him in some future combination of us.

Kelcee was usually the first to breakfast. At worst, she'd come down second. She always came fully dressed, always took cream and two sugars in her coffee, and always hugged everyone. She called Erin "Mom" whenever she was over. My mother was always referred to as Ms. Powell. If my hair was braided, she'd always greet me in the morning by playing with it. This annoyed Mom to no end, and Kelcee did it deliberately.

"Stop trying to mark your territory," Mom said to her.

"I am merely admiring my girlfriend's handiwork," she replied.

"You're growing your hair out, Kelcee," Erin said. "Are you jealous of someone?"

She laughed. "Yes, I am, Mom. Not giving up my spot in the bed to the new kid just yet."

"She can keep mine warm," Joey said through a mouthful of toast.

"Like I'd want to smell your rank ass every night. I've got my own bed," I said, winking at him.

"I know where you sleep," Angie grinned. "We can always drag you back to our room in handcuffs."

Mom gave Angie a swat on her back. "I don't know why you have handcuffs, but you will not be using them on my daughter. Do I make myself clear?"

"Yes, Ms. Powell, Angie and Kelcee said promptly.

Hannah was reading the morning paper. She sat it down for a moment. "I can explain the handcuffs if you want to know, Tina."

"I do not need them explained, thank you very much." There was something hard to read in the way she replied. It wasn't cold or angry. Perhaps it was resignation at the path I was taking. "Angie, were you going to camp out at the pond next weekend? I need to know so I can tell Robert not to show up and discover you three doing some ungodly mischief.”

“Weather permitting, yes.” She smiled at Joey. “I would think a young biologist could learn a great deal from observing us in the wild.”

Kelcee giggled. “Watching us will scar the poor boy for life. Do keep him home, Ms. Powell.”

“I intend to! There will be no research papers being turned in on your mating habits if I have any say in the matter.”

Kelcee giggled. “Angie tried doing that once for biology class, but Mr. Hill wouldn’t allow it.”

“I did hear about that one at parent-teacher conferences,” Erin mumbled through her cereal.

“I don’t get it,” I said. “If you all kept quiet, you could have your ménage à trois and nobody would be the wiser.”

“We love Angie,” Joey smiled. “That’s never going to be a ticket to anonymity.”

“She brings the crazy to our mundane existences and makes us love life in a way we never did before meeting her. But you already knew that, didn’t you? Tick, tick, tick.”

I suddenly blushed. “Something you want to tell me, Sarah?” Mom asked.

“Absolutely not!”

“Sarah, you’re going to be a writer. Suppose you pull off writing a novel while in high school. Everyone is going to know and remember you. You are never going to hide from the world if that happens. Everything you say and do might be scrutinized.

That's going to make dating Robert hard enough. Double dating is the way to go. No orgies under the bleachers. Got it?"

"Understood," they said. Angie appeared like she wanted to say something, but Kelcee stared at her, and she held her tongue.

A few days later, our lawyer, Chandra, was out at the house to see us. As Hannah and I were both writing novels, Chandra had to handle various legal matters to ensure copyright protection. Erin wanted to make sure she'd drawn up everything properly in the contract Mom and I had signed, making her my agent as well as Hannah's. Finally, Dad was going to be released from jail by the end of August. Even my idiot father eventually figured out that behaving behind bars would get him out sooner. He was going to be living in our old home by himself. Mom wanted to make sure he didn't come anywhere near us and sought to make that very clear to him.

"Part of his conditions of release are that he has no contact with either of you," Chandra said. "If either of you sees him, you need to call the police immediately. I would let the high school know as soon as you can of the situation, so they don't allow him on campus or let him pick Sarah up by claiming to be a custodial parent."

"I'll get on that immediately," Mom said. "Eldon hasn't indicated there's been anything amiss with him lately, though he was talking about harming us shortly after he was sentenced. The jail dealt with him at that time, and he assumed the danger had passed. I don't buy that, but I can't prove Eldon is wrong."

"Would he have any access to weapons that you know of?"

"He never owned any when we were married. I don't think Eldon owns any, but I can't be sure."

Hannah shook her head. "Dad was very firm on that. God was the only protection he needed. He stuck to fishing. He never hunted. I highly doubt there would be any guns in that house at all."

"That's something, at least. Let's hope Daniel goes away quietly." Chandra sighed. "I have the feeling he won't. He seems to be the type that wants the last word, and you all need to be on your guard."

Later that night, Mom was in the common area of our rooms in the guest wing, having a cup of tea and reading a book. I sat down next to her and poured myself a cup.

"Why would Dad come after us for leaving him if he was so miserable with us in the first place? He could at least start over and make something of himself now."

"He could, if he wanted to. Get out of Michigan, move somewhere where no one knows him, and reinvent himself. Maybe go back into preaching." Mom laughed at that thought. "You know our kind. Nothing gives us a thrill like a good story of repentance and rededication to God's work. We want to believe anything is possible with God and the worst sinner can be saved, so we'll give him the chance to prove God right."

I shook my head. "That has disaster written all over it."

"Probably," she said. "Some other woman will become his victim. He won't tell her about us. Not the truth, anyway." She paused. "I think the answer you're looking for is his pride. He would never consider us his equals. He was superior to us in every way, and we rejected him by not following his will and guidance. That's going to eat at him. He's suffered because of his actions, but he's likely to place that blame on our heads rather than his own. The more success we have, the angrier he will be. We've moved on to a better life. He's in jail."

CHAPTER 29

Robert turned fifteen on July 17th. Our group had a party for him at the Pizza Hut in South Lyon, where we ate a lot, gave the birthday boy gifts we could afford on our allowances, and rejoiced that the youngest group member had aged up at last.

For me, the birthday party Robert's family threw was more important. His Grandpa and Grandma Hill would be there, and Robert wanted them to meet me. Since Angie's role in our relationship wasn't set yet, nothing would be said of her for the moment. The family was also rather abuzz with the news that Brenda was pregnant. Grandma Hill was none too pleased with this. Robert said to pay it no mind.

"Grandma is like this every time someone in the family gets pregnant. Doesn't matter who it is or how old they are; she's just naturally crabby, like my sister. She'll come around and like the baby once it's born."

Grandpa Hill was just like Jerry. He adored me and proudly welcomed me into the family, even though I had just started dating his grandson.

"Most of the time, when a man of the Hill clan finds someone he likes, he'll settle down quickly and love the object of his desire with all his heart. If Robert's chosen you, that means something powerful," Grandpa said. I noted with interest that he didn't say "woman." There must be a same sex couple or two in the Hill family tree somewhere.

"Hmph," Jerry said. "You didn't approve when I picked Brenda!"

"You two said you'd marry each other when you were six," Grandma grumbled. "That you never even considered anyone else was silly and stupid, and we objected. You should have at least looked around. It worked out well for you in the end, though I fear Robert is taking after you, Jerry."

"I found someone I like a lot," Robert said, grasping me by the hand and smiling.

I wore one of my business casual outfits Mom had bought for me. I wanted to appear professional and someone they would like their grandson to be dating. Grandma Hill eyed me studiously. "You dress like you are trying to convince me you work downtown at the bank," she mused. "Trying to be older than you are."

"I'm writing my first novel," I said. "That's not a bad description of who I am at the moment."

"A novelist!" Grandpa clapped his hands excitedly. "What genre are you writing?"

"Supernatural thriller/romance," I said proudly.

"Splendid! Splendid! How many pages have you written so far?"

"332, sir," I replied.

"Very good! Keep at it!"

Grandma Hill was chomping at the bit to say something, but Grandpa's enthusiasm seemed to have cut her off. Liz nodded at her knowingly. "She's got that otherworldly charm that can make a young man forget his senses. Comes from hanging out with demons," she grumbled.

"Sarah is the first woman my age I've met who can appreciate the things I like and accept me as I am, even if that means putting up with looking through telescopes and holding turtles. She's a writer, not a scientist. But she loves me for who I am, even if I'm a little nerdy around the edges. I'm never going to be rich as a teacher. She doesn't care. She sees something in me that makes her happy, and she brings joy to my life. That's not how a demon would see the world. Maybe it explains why you've never found anyone you like, Liz. You don't even have the heart to make another person happy. You can't even be happy yourself."

Liz was furious at her brother's denunciation of her. I expected Grandma Hill to rip into him. To my surprise, she cackled with glee at his outburst. "What is this? My grandson has some fire in his veins! When did this happen?"

Brenda smiled at her son. "He's grown up a lot this year."

"Yes, he has. Robert, I don't take anything I said back. I am a stubborn old mule, and admitting I'm wrong is a thing I avoid like the plague. I didn't think you had any fight in you at all. I am glad to see there are things in this world you value enough to raise your voice over. You will need that in life. Liz, I am proud of you, and I have your back, but stop yanking your brother's chain. You might regret it now that he's figured out that he has the power to yank back." Grandma glanced over at me. "And why do you love my grandson?"

"He has taught me a great deal about the world, as has his father. I'm no longer the innocent I was before I came here, raised on lies and fairy tales and taught to believe men had the right to make me obey them. Robert is nothing like my father. I can trust him to treat me with love and respect. He brings calm and stability to my world. My aunt's a millionaire. I don't know if I'll ever be able to match her success. If all I ever manage to be in life is a housewife, I'm going to be there at Robert's side, raising our children. If I do become a writer, I'll be the best writer I can. He'll help me achieve that, and I'll brag about him to the world. He will never be just a teacher in my eyes. Just like Jerry isn't just a teacher in your eyes. Right, Brenda?"

Brenda smiled and hugged Jerry. "He's been my best friend since forever. Every day, I wake up to his snoring, and I still think I'm the luckiest woman alive."

"There's who you model, Sarah," Grandpa Hill said. "Not that lousy excuse for a human being that got your mother pregnant. You be like Jerry and Brenda, and you'll make us proud, even if we're looking down on you from the stars. Am I right, Bernice?"

"They have been good for each other," Grandma Hill said, nodding her head. "Though I feel like you should have offered us as a comparison, too."

"You are a sour old grump. Thankfully, you're a firecracker in the sack, so I put up with your foolishness."

"Best your wrinkled old ass will ever get!"

Now I understood how they'd managed to stay married. "Is Jerry your only child?"

"Nope," Jerry said. "I'm the youngest of four brothers."

"Each one is as different as the last," Grandma said. "Michael is a farmer, Larry is a police detective, and George splits time between Paris and New York as a fashion designer."

"But we all get along splendidly," Jerry said. "Always have."

"Makes me jealous, actually," Brenda said. "My family is very austere and doesn't show a lot of affection. I swear I spent more time with Jerry's family than I did my own because I craved that sense of togetherness and affection they had. Even though they were very different personalities, they accepted and encouraged each other. To this day, his brothers see me as their little sister. Jerry? I don't know what it was, but we just knew we wanted to be together from the beginning."

"I see them in you and Robert," Grandpa Hill said warmly. "You two look at each other in the same way."

"They won't be like the two of you," Liz grinned wickedly. "They have their own little secrets."

"What if they do?" Jerry growled. "They have a right to make their own way in the world, just like you do."

"They do," Liz said. "I'm curious to see how they manage."

When it was time for them to go, Grandpa Hill gave me a big hug. "I hope I see you again."

"Me, too!" Grandma didn't react at all. I walked over to her. "I hope we can get along going forward. I love Robert. I really do."

"Remember that when you fight," she said. "Remember that when you get so frustrated with him, you want to hop a bus to anywhere and leave him behind. He will let you down, but you'll let him down, too. My Edward can be a damned fool sometimes, but I've never met anyone else who could hold a candle to him."

I took a chance and hugged her. "If I marry Robert someday, I hope you're alive to say that as a wedding toast."

She cracked a smile. "You'd let me do that, would you? What a foolishly brave thing to say." She accepted that hug all the same. "You'd fit in this family, I think. If it ever comes to that."

After they left, Brenda gave me a playful hug. "She accepted you! And on the first meeting, too!"

"She wouldn't let me hug her until I was ten," Robert laughed.

"I got one at five!" Liz playfully teased him.

"You're as sour as she is. No surprise she likes you best of all her grandchildren," Jerry needled her. "Two porcupines who love flexing their quills together."

"Two realists in a family full of dreamers and dingbats," Liz laughed.

"And yet you obviously love each other," I said.

Liz smiled at her father. "We do, don't we? That's just how the Hills are. I'm not going to hug you, though."

"Ever?" I asked.

"Oh, I'll hug you one day. I'm going to wait and see if you break my brother's heart. If you don't, I'll let him keep you."

***

As the days passed and my novel grew closer to completion, Angie would seek me out to ask how the story was going. I'd settled on the working title of *Shadowfall*, symbolic as it was of a small town gradually falling under the shadow of a powerful demon. Angie and I would lie on my bed, and I'd tell her the latest developments and where I thought the story would go.

"When your novel is finished, what happens to our characters? I do have a personal investment in my demon, Ashley," she said.

I chuckled. "I just took some things from the two of us in making Ashley and Mary's characters. Ashley isn't totally you. There's a lot of Hannah in her, too."

"Who do you think taught me the finer points of life?" Angie laughed. "Ashley is mine, and you can't convince me otherwise. Oh, and you got the ending wrong. You should fix that."

"I did not! It is exactly the way I want it. Mary chooses Ashley's demonic life over her own as an exorcist. It must be that way."

Angie shook her head. "What happens to Mary when she does that?"

"She becomes a demon. Not right away, but gradually. All Ashley's thralls follow the same path."

"And that's where you're wrong," Angie said with a smile. "That's what they think will happen, but Mary isn't like the other people Ashley turns. Mary's personality is too powerful. Just as knowing Ashley changes Mary's view of the world, knowing Mary is going to change Ashley. Ashley will pick up some of her sense of compassion, justice, and goodness. She will become something new and different, and she and Mary will attempt to form a kingdom based on the best of both of their worlds. Thralls are mostly disposable. They're a source of food and entertainment. Ashley will never see Mary in that way. If Mary saw Ashley's true form, could she still love her? Ashley and Mary's journey to understanding themselves and what they want their world to be is the subject of your second book. Your third book is what happens when Heaven and Hell realize Ashley and Mary pose a threat to both of their empires. Give the publisher more content, and they'll be in a bigger hurry to sign you if they like what they see."

My jaw dropped. She understood my characters better than I did. "How did you do that?"

She smiled at me. "I am your demon. I should know how she thinks. I know how much you are changing me, and it takes my breath away. Ashley will feel the same way. Maybe to the point where she'll allow Mary to keep her humanity if that's what she chooses. A marriage of Heaven and Hell, destined to try and forge a third kingdom on Earth."

"If I never sell a single book in my life, I will write that trilogy so that we can share it." I kissed her. "All I want is for you to be with me."

"That's what I want, too," she replied. She returned my kiss and snuggled up close to me. "But you will sell a lot of books, and people will argue over what level of Hell you belong in. Of that, I have no doubt."

"I suddenly have so many things running through my head. I need to write them down. I just don't want to let you go right now."

Angie smiled. "I'm tempting fate by being here. I don't become your lover until a later chapter of our book. Right now, you need to concentrate on writing."

I knew she was right. I let her leave my room without stopping her. That won't last forever. I can't be without her. She has become both my muse and my demon.

CHAPTER 30

The study group was at the pond on a late July day. We'd finished lunch and were feeling rather lazy. Melanie, Yuki, and Lucy wanted to sunbathe. I didn't mind the idea, but I wanted to go swimming, and so did Dee and Angie. The guys were all in favor of swimming. I thought we had sorted the situation out until Dan had to go and open his mouth.

"Who is singing today?"

"Nobody's singing today, dummy! The bet is over." Yuki laughed.

"No big deal. All we would have to do is make a new bet," Dan smiled.

"I had my turn. Someone else can strip this time," she replied.

"Are you trying to get me out of my clothes already?" Melanie laughed. "We've only just started dating! That's a bit much!"

Dan blushed at the suggestion. "I didn't say you."

"We should totally make him do it, though!" Yuki said.

"Sing 'Old MacDonald Had a Farm', but with every verse, he takes off something!" Lucy squealed with delight at the idea.

"Not going to happen," Dan said.

Angie hadn't been there when we'd sung, so I had to explain the context to her. She smiled, nodded, and then entered the fray herself. "For someone who talked so big, Dan, you sure turned tail and ran quickly enough. I'll sing anything you want naked. I'm not afraid."

Melanie sighed. "You're missing the point. We're daring each other to do things that make us a little bit uncomfortable. Being naked in front of everyone else is another level entirely— nobody wants to go that far. Nobody sane anyway. You exist on another level entirely."

"Do I? Let's take a poll." Angie looked around at all of us. "Let's jump two summers into the future. You just finished your junior year. You're all up here at the pond hanging out. You're all still as good of friends as you are now. You're still dating the person you're dating. If you could get naked and swim here—just swim and sunbathe. No sex or anything like that. Would you do it? Raise your hands if you would."

Everyone in the group raised their hands. Even Yuki, to our utter amazement. Nobody said anything for a while. Finally, it was Dee who spoke, and she grasped Chad's hand as she began. "I'm curious about it. I might want to try it next summer. That may be a step Chad and I are willing to take. Let's put it to the side now, but bring it back up next summer and at least discuss it as a group."

Melanie grasped Dan's hand. "I think I'll second that motion. Let's see how we feel about it then."

"Works for me," he said. "How about you, Yuki?"

Yuki looked out at the dock. "If you would have asked me last year if I'd ever have the courage to strip down to my underwear and sing in front of all of you, I would have called you idiots. I did it, though. I wasn't going to let Sarah take my punishment alone. When I was done, I didn't feel ashamed like I thought I would. Nobody was staring at me. We all had fun. Maybe I could handle sunbathing naked. Maybe I'd really enjoy it. I don't know."

"When I'm sixteen, I'm totally skinny-dipping!" Lucy blurted out.

"I think it's settled then. We'll discuss it in the spring when we make our summer plans," Melanie said. "Nobody does anything they don't want. There's not going to be anything sexual involved. It's just us as friends spending time together however we wish."

I realized just how many of our friends' wishes were beginning to match ours. Angie had chosen this group of friends for me. Had she known we would all find ourselves here one day?

***

The end came for the threesome of Joey, Kelcee, and Angie as they knew it would. Joey moved up north to Houghton for school in August. I wasn't there when they said goodbye. Angie and Kelcee didn't talk much about it either. They carried on as a couple like nothing had happened, but their actions didn't fool anyone. They missed him. I decided to stay out of their way unless they invited me to be part of their activities.

Kelcee was very up-front with me. "Angie and I are going to try to make a go of things as a couple for right now. I'm not sure how that's going to go."

"You don't think it is going to work?"

She sighed. "I haven't a clue. Joey is having second thoughts about dating other people. Angie is all over the place. She wants us to be together. She wants to bring you in. She wants to bring Robert in. I'm not ready to bring someone new in, even if I do think you're interesting."

"If Angie makes a pass at me, what do you want me to do?" I asked.

"That's between the two of you. I know she has feelings for you. I also would like to think you respect me as a friend and wouldn't stab me in the back."

Now I was confused. "We've talked about having sex together…"

"Yes, we have." She lazily traced her finger down my nose and across my lips. "Talking is one thing. Acting on those feelings is another. You need to worry about your relationship with Robert right now. Whatever happens with Angie and me will happen. If we break up, then you can have her, and the three of you can go do your own thing. My endgame is Joey. If Angie comes with us, then my life is better."

"Sounds good to me." I hugged her, maybe a little tighter than I should have. She didn't object. "If I ever got the chance to be with the two of you, though…I'd take it."

"Saucy bitch!" she laughed. "Careful what you wish for. Unlike Angie, I don't feel the need to wait for Robert to do anything. If you flirt too hard with me, I'll steal your first time for myself." She slapped me on the butt and let me go. Teasing Kelcee was something that I wasn't sure I wanted to do for a while.

Mom and Charli were getting together once a week now. Sometimes they would go out, but it was equally as likely that Charli would have dinner with us. They regularly discussed English literature and poetry. Mom was struggling to find her voice as a writer, and Charli was there to encourage her to try different things and see what worked for her. They loved going out to the pond for a swim, and Hannah and Erin often went along. Angie and I were not invited. This was adult swim, they said. It was clear when they came back, they'd had a few drinks and were in a relaxed mood. Charli wasn't afraid to knock back a few beers, and Mom always made sure one of the empty rooms in our wing was prepared in case Charli needed to sleep the booze off before she drove home. Only once had she needed to avail herself of it, and she was very apologetic about it afterward.

On that particular morning, the coffee pot in our wing was already up and running. I was on my second cup, sitting in the chair by the window, and writing story ideas in a notebook to show Angie later. I didn't dress up if I was in our wing and I knew Robert wasn't going to be around. I was just wearing a camisole and panties. Charli wandered out of her room in an ill-fitting sleep shirt and headed straight for the coffee pot. She poured herself a cup and took a few sips before she realized I was there. She blushed.

"Good morning," she groaned. "I guess I fucked up last night. This is weird, you know. Please don't tell anyone."

I smiled at her. "Not used to seeing students this early in the morning?"

"I woke up, and my clothes were missing."

"Mom said she had to throw them in the wash because you got drunk and fell in the pond. She didn't think you wanted to smell like fish first thing in the morning."

"What's your excuse? You didn't fall in the pond."

"This is my house. I don't need to get dressed up if I don't want to. Besides, you're dating my mom. I won't be surprised to see you at breakfast if things continue to go well in the future."

"I'll have fun explaining that to the school board," she mumbled and sipped on her coffee. She sat down in the chair opposite me. It was very clear Mom had thrown everything of hers in the wash. The shirt she'd found for Charli must have been one of Angie's. It fit very tightly around her chest because Angie's was smaller.

"There's probably a robe in the closet," I said. "I doubt Mom would want you coming down to breakfast dressed like that."

Charli blushed even harder. "Nipples much."

"I'm not one of those 'hot for teacher' types, so you're safe," I said. "Though I don't mind the view. I'm partial to Angie's, though."

Mom picked this minute to wander into the room. She shook her head. "I really need to stock your room with clothes that properly fit you."

"She could use a robe," I smiled. "She's a bit self-conscious."

"I'm glad someone in this house is! I'll grab one of mine. Stay here. If Hannah sees you in that, I'm going to have to mop the drool off the kitchen floor."

"We didn't do anything last night, did we? I know I kissed you a couple of times…"

"You kissed my mom?" I shouted.

"She kisses a lot better than Daniel, I must say." Mom grinned at Charli. "I might actually like this lesbian thing you all do."

Charli and I giggled at this. "You make it sound like I am having this conversation with my grandmother rather than my girlfriend. Still, I'm amazed she let me kiss her. She's pretty good at it herself."

"What happened to taking it slow, you two?"

"Too much champagne will do that," Mom sighed. "A momentary lapse of judgement. I don't regret it, though. Not one bit."

Mom paused for a moment. I realized why as soon as it happened. She was enjoying looking at Charli. Everything had gone in the wash, including her underwear. It was very clear she was braless, and Mom suddenly realized her mind liked what she saw. Then Charli smiled at her. "Are you ogling me, Ms. Powell?"

"I'm not hot for teacher, but I think someone in this house is," I chuckled.

Mom blushed furiously. "Take it slow, get her a robe, don't stare…" she muttered.

"You're allowed to look, Tina. I give you permission. I like that you're interested in me."

"It's the first time I've looked at you and felt…lust."

Charli smiled. "It's okay. That's normal for people to be attracted to each other. You'll grow into it if this is what you decide you want going forward."

The two of them exchanged a warm hug. Mom needed reassurance in that moment, and Charli surrounded her in love and acceptance. Then Mom scurried off to find her a robe and return the world to proper decorum.

***

A few days before school started, Mom got a phone call that Dad had been released from jail. The terms of his parole were very specific: he was not under any circumstances to have contact with us without permission of the court.

He went to live with Grandpa and Grandma for a few days before moving back into our old home in Melvindale. But Dad was not idle—Grandpa put him to work around the church, vacuuming carpets and trimming bushes. Dad enjoyed his freedom at first, but then he became troublesome. The time by himself caused him to start brooding. He'd spend long hours reading the Bible, praying, and fasting. He let his appearance go, and he began to look disheveled. He'd talk to himself when he assumed no one was listening. Grandpa immediately pulled him out of the house and back under their roof to keep an eye on him. Grandpa's pride was never in short supply, but he knew trouble when he saw it. He called our lawyer, Chandra, and told her things weren't going well. Chandra immediately contacted Dad's parole officer and the courts.

CHAPTER 31

Summer vacation was almost over. Robert was making one of his last visits to survey the grounds, though he said he'd be out on weekends when he could continue to observe things as summer changed to fall and fall to winter.

"New things turn up all the time," he said as we ate lunch on the picnic table together. "Birds fly south and leave us behind. They'll be replaced by other birds from further north who are looking for a vacation somewhere a little less arctic. The reptiles and some of the mammals will hibernate. It will be quieter here, but life will go on, and I want to watch it."

I had to smile. He was already sounding like a schoolteacher. I knew all this in general terms, but I let him talk. This would be good practice for him. I wonder if he'll have to make the same rules for teaching our children in his classes as Jerry did. It was still warm. The sky looked a bit unsettled, as we were expecting thunderstorms later in the day. Everything seemed to be signaling that change was on the way. Now was the time, and yet I found myself suddenly terrified. Why? We'd seen each other naked. Now would be the perfect time for our first skinny-dipping excursion.

He sensed something was off. "What is it?"

"I so want to rip my clothes off and dive in right now."

"But you're scared, right?"

I nodded. "I feel like I've been trying to do too much. I love you and Angie. I really do. I want to be a person you're excited about loving back…"

Robert put his arm around me. "You already are. Angie would say so, too."

"But she does things to me that get me excited. So do you."

"And it's addicting. We're fifteen. The idea of us being lovers? Shit, I can't wait! But waiting isn't bad. You need to know you're ready. So do I. You aren't, are you?"

I shook my head. "That's the thing about the book I'm writing. I can't give away my beliefs and morals and still be happy with myself, and neither can my character. A demon and an exorcist fall in love with each other. The exorcist doesn't want to simply become a demon. The demon doesn't want to become a saint—anything but that! They admire qualities in each other that make them better individuals and happier, bringing them closer together. I'm afraid of surrendering myself too soon. That's what started this whole mess. Angie and Kelcee were too young when they started their threesome. They're only starting to figure life out now when Joey's getting ready to leave. If I'm not able to make my own life make sense, how do I write a book that's any good? How do I become a partner that's going to make any relationship we have succeed?"

Robert nodded at me. "It's not going to rain for a while. If we just swim in our clothes, we should dry off under the sun. And if we don't, so what? Your mom's not going to get mad that you got your clothes wet. She'll love that you came to a place in your life where you had to make a choice, and you chose the correct option. She's afraid you'll grow up to be like Angie. So are you."

He could be so earnest at times. I loved him…and yet I knew he was just as mischievous as I was, and sex with him was going to be so much fun. He was feeling everything I was feeling. He just hid it better than I did. He wanted the best for me, even if that meant he was forced to wait to get something he truly wanted.

"What color underwear did you pick today?" I asked him.

"I was in a hurry. White."

"That's dull. I'm wearing white, too. I didn't think I'd wimp out and want to stay dressed."

Robert smiled at me. "We've already seen everything. If we show through a little, it won't be the end of the world."

That's how our last swim of the year happened…Robert in his briefs, and me sporting a very unsexy bra and panties. It didn't matter. We just had fun being together and making normal teenage memories, even if in an unorthodox way. Angie, Kelcee, and Joey did what they did as much for the thrill as for the relationship. They fell in love as part of the game, but I'm not sure they ever found something lasting where the three of them would always want to be together. If my destiny turns out to be Mrs. Sarah Hill, wife of high school teacher Robert Hill, there will be no regrets on my part. I'm just willing to keep the door open to something bigger and bolder.

The rest of August was a blur. I spent most of it writing from dawn until dusk, knowing I would be extremely limited in the amount of time I could devote to writing because of homework. When September came, I'd be just another student. My teachers wouldn't care about my novel. Homework always comes first. Such is the way of the world, and it always has been. Hannah was now reading my dailies and coaching me on how to improve them. On August 25th, I wrote the last chapter of the first volume. Two days of read-throughs and edits followed. I printed it all out and dropped it on Hannah's desk.

"It's finished," I said.

She dialed a long-distance number on her phone and waited for the person on the other end to pick up. She hit a button on the phone and turned on the speaker.

"Hi, Tracy! _Shadowfall_ is done. I'm sending it to you by courier tomorrow."

"Seriously? She finished it?"

"Of course, she finished it. She is my niece. We Brenners don't fuck around when it comes to writing."

I snickered. "Are you her editor?"

"Tracy Cole, at your service. One day, I may be your editor, too. I'm not sure what will happen. You've told her the odds are she'll get refused. We don't publish writers this young."

"And I told you I'm willing to accept co-author status if that's what it takes to get her foot in the door." My jaw dropped. I didn't realize she would go that far.

"I've only read the blurbs you've shared. Those are outstanding for a teenager to write, but is the whole thing that way?"

"It will need some work, but her English teacher and I have been doing a lot of editing work with her, and hopefully that will make the process easier for you."

"Hannah, the last thing I need in my life right now is more work! I've got your next novel in the pipeline!"

"Then get someone else to do it. Just read it. You promised me that much."

"I will read it. You know I will. I just can't promise you any more than that."

"I know," Hannah said. "Have I ever sent you anything shitty in my entire life?"

"You've sent me stuff we didn't use," Tracy laughed. "And there was that time you were drunk as fuck and sent me a synopsis about a man who falls in love with a gerbil…"

I could barely contain myself. Hannah was horrified.

"You promised **never** to speak of that!"

"Sarah should know Felicity Parr is far from perfect. None of you writers are. I've never once gotten a submission from anyone I didn't have to fix up, argue over, demand rewrites on, or set on fire to kill it. We editors make sure your asses don't smell like shit, and we make it look like you passed English top of the class and didn't sleep through it. So be nice to us and buy us presents when you make it in print. Am I clear?"

"Yes, ma'am!"

Hannah sent the manuscript off the next morning. I wondered what Tracy would say when she read it. My friends knew I'd submitted my manuscript, and I was nervously waiting for news. We knew what she said, too. It was a long shot that I'd get accepted. Lucy was over at the house two days before school started, hanging out with me. She saw how nervous I was and gave me a huge hug. Angie was there and joined in the hug.

"It's a shame these necklaces don't actually have magic powers in them," Lucy sighed. "I'd cast a spell for your success."

Angie walked over and kissed the necklaces, making sure she kissed Lucy on the neck in the process. "I'm a demon. I grant you temporary use of my powers for the purpose of bringing Sarah success."

"As if that would work!" Lucy laughed.

"It may not, but I was able to peek down your blouse. Nice bra!" Angie giggled.

"By all the powers holy and unholy, may the universe bend to my will and grant unto Sarah success as an author…and smite this unholy perverted demon in the process!"

"By my power, so mote it be," Angie said somberly. "Except for the smiting the demon bit."

Thankfully, Mom didn't wander in at that moment. She'd move us out of this house if she thought demons really lived here. It was all just a story I'd written. It had no power to change the real world.

***

Robert's great project to map Hannah's grounds was complete for the season. Hannah had brought someone from the Michigan Department of Agriculture out to tour the grounds and discuss ways to preserve and protect the land she owned. Many of those old fruit trees we found could be saved with proper pruning and fertilization. She'd also let her colleagues at the University of Michigan's Conservation Ecology department know she had land they might want to use to give their students hands-on practice in their studies. The notes of a certain student from South Lyon High School were suddenly being read by real scientists and academics. Robert Hill suddenly showed up on their radar as a young man they might want to keep tabs on in the future, and Jerry got to show his son off to Hannah's colleagues. I was so proud of him.

In the end, the decision to put Mom in charge of Hannah's house brought one complication none of us foresaw. She picked up the phone when it rang and answered, "Brenner residence, how may I direct your call?" just as she usually did. The person on the other end of the line was my father. He'd gotten into Grandpa's desk and found Hannah's contact information. He was trying to start trouble with Hannah, but he instantly recognized his ex-wife's voice on the other end.

"So, this is where you've been hiding," he said. "I should have guessed."

"You're not allowed to contact me. Hang up now, or I'll call the police."

"I'll hang up," he said. "But this isn't over."

"It is over. I want nothing more to do with you ever." Mom hung up on him. She ran and got Hannah, who called Chandra and then the police in short order.

We'd been outed. Now the question was, what was Dad going to do next?

CHAPTER 32

We had a cookout at Hannah's on Labor Day. Jerry and Brenda were invited and were bringing Robert. Charli was coming, too. We all gathered in the yard and were enjoying our meal when we noticed a car speeding down our driveway. Mom recognized it at once. It was Grandpa Brenner's. It squealed to a stop next to the house, and Dad jumped out. Dark circles under his eyes and several days' beard growth covered his face. His clothes were rumpled, and his right hand was covered in dried blood. Erin quickly called the sheriff. None of us moved at first, save for Hannah, who walked over to meet him.

"You're not supposed to be here!" she snapped. "Get out now before the cops get you!"

"Shut up, you whore! I'm not here to see you. I'm here for Christina and Sarah. It's time they came home."

"They left you," Hannah said. "You were divorced. You have no claim here." She snapped her fingers and pointed to the road. "Be gone, Daniel!"

Mom was seated at the picnic table. She suddenly stood up and walked over to Hannah's side. "You had two decades of marriage to show you loved me, and you refused to do it. You treated Sarah and me with utter contempt and viciousness. Why would we ever come back to you?"

"Because God demands your obedience!" Dad shouted.

Mom did something I never expected. She laughed at him. "When did you ever obey God, Daniel? Where was the tenderness and kindness of Jesus in you? You never were a good shepherd or a loving husband."

"No man worth his salt would ever take you. You'll be alone for the rest of your life!" Dad shouted.

"Maybe I've already found someone better than you!" Mom blurted out. "I don't know! There's so much I don't know! But I'll never go back to living with you! Ever!"

Charli was genuinely stunned. Under the most trying circumstances possible, Mom peeked out of the closet and told her how she felt.

Dad stared at me. "What of you, Sarah? Are you going to stay in this den of iniquity, too? Do you not care for your own soul?"

"Like you would know the way to heaven, Dad," I said from my seat on the picnic table. "All those Bible verses you taught me, and you never took a single one to heart."

"You pushed your daughter so much, she's lost most of her faith," Mom said sternly. "Aren't you proud? What a fine preacher you turned out to be!"

"I will fix this!" he said, sounding just a bit unsure of himself.

"There's nothing to fix!" I said. "I'm happy with who I am! I'm going to be a writer like Hannah. I'm in love. I can't wait to see what the future has for me, but it isn't going to be with you. You're a past I want to bury forever!"

"Tell me that to my face!"

I got up and walked over to stand by Mom and Hannah. Suddenly, I felt Angie and Robert beside me, each holding a hand to steady me. Erin had joined Hannah. Charli ran up to join Mom, and Robert's parents stood beside him. In the distance, we could hear sirens.

"This is our family," Hannah said proudly. "We will take care of Tina and Sarah from now on. Now if I were you, I'd get in that car and run like hell, or you'll be back staring at the same gray bars you left."

The sirens were louder now. Dad ran for the car. It was too late for him, though. A Washtenaw County Sheriff's car rolled into the driveway, and Dad knew he was caught. He raised his hands and was meekly taken into custody once more. It was worse than we realized. Dad had assaulted Grandpa and stolen his car to drive to the mansion—he would be facing a new string of charges.

The police interviewed Mom for about thirty minutes while Dad sat in the back of the patrol car. Unlike the emotional mess she was in last year when Dad beat her up, Mom was firmly in control today. She answered the officer's questions dispassionately, explained everything that happened, and carried herself with authority and pride. Charli was beside her throughout the questioning, and it was a beautiful thing to watch.

Robert and I played frisbee in the yard while all this was going on. Robert suggested it to calm me down, but I found Dad was watching us from his seat in the back of the patrol car. He was yelling something at me, but I couldn't hear it, and I didn't care. Living a normal life was the best revenge, and ignoring his outbursts just made him feel more powerless. I wanted him to feel that uselessness. He'd made us feel that way for so many years.

Angie came over to join us, with Robert throwing the frisbee to each of us in turn. At some point, Angie figured out her presence seemed to annoy my father even more. She'd hug me, blow kisses at Robert, and go out of her way to act silly. She was closer to the police car than I was, and she could hear him better than I could. Finally, she walked over to the police car with a frisbee in hand.

"God, don't you ever shut up?" she yelled at him. "Nobody's going to hear you screaming in Hell except us demons, and we love to hear your misery. I've half a mind to drag you there myself."

Dad stopped yelling. He didn't know what to say. He just glowered at Angie.

"Your daughter is going to be an author," Angie said. "So is your wife. They are going to be amazing at it, I think. You tried so hard to stop them, but you just made them more determined. You failed at everything you tried to do in your life. You'll spend forever screaming about it, and we demons will dance around your miserable soul and mock you. You'll see my face in Hell, Mr. Brenner. I'll be waiting for you!" She blew him a kiss and then walked back to rejoin us.

"You don't believe in hell," Robert said.

"He does. If I can give him a nightmare or two, that's payback for hurting someone I love."

With their interviews concluded, the deputies said their farewells and drove Dad away. It was time to return him to custody. I didn't think much of it as the patrol car left. As it turned out, that would be the last day I saw my father alive. Two days after he was arrested, he hung himself in his jail cell.

263

CHAPTER 33

My father was buried in the Brenner family plot. Grandpa threatened not to give him a headstone and let him lie in an unmarked grave, but Grandma overruled him. An assistant pastor officiated at the funeral. Mom, Hannah, and I went. Robert begged to go along, and after thinking it over, Mom gave her approval. It was the first time Hannah had seen her family since Mom married Daniel. Grandpa hugged her when he saw her, something she wasn't expecting but tearfully accepted. Grandpa and Grandma hugged Mom and me and said they were thankful to God we weren't harmed. We were grateful Grandpa was alive and rejoiced in that together. Grandpa's head was bandaged up. Dad had hit him with a chair when his back was turned. The ending was bad, but it could have been so much worse.

Grandma was never one to turn down the opportunity to make things uncomfortable, and she asked who Robert was. When I said he was my boyfriend, she eyed him carefully, and I sensed he was about to be grilled.

"Sarah says you've been married a very long time," Robert said, catching her off guard. "I want to treat her as she deserves to be treated. What advice would you give me?"

Silver-tongued devil! Grandma Brenner loved giving unsolicited advice. For someone to ask her opinion was a moment of bliss, and she talked to Robert and me for fifteen minutes about how Grandpa wooed her and the way they learned how to treat each other when they were a young married couple. There was a lot of religion involved. With Grandma, there always would be. No doubt about it, though—they loved each other dearly, and that love was something we felt in her words. She never got around to asking if Robert was a Christian. Somehow, he seemed so respectful and kind, she took it for granted that Sarah Brenner would ever choose a heathen. There would be more battles with the Brenner family in the future, but on this day, we all came together to bury my father, and we did so in peace.

I asked Grandpa if Dad left a note before he took his life. Grandpa nodded. "He did. No, I won't tell you what it said. He was hateful and cruel and jealous of your happiness. That could have been his had he chosen a better path in life. I never taught him to behave that way. Your father was a wicked man who deceived us all for a time. He has gotten his reward. He will never see paradise."

This was disingenuous. Grandpa and Grandma had taught him his beliefs and his fondness for patriarchy and toxic religion. That the plant they painstakingly nurtured grew wild as it got older didn't absolve them of guilt in my eyes. Dad went too far. That was on him. They pushed him in the wrong direction. I sounded off about this in the car on the way home from the funeral. Robert listened supportively. Hannah didn't say anything. It was Mom who finally interrupted my rant.

"Sounds like someone else I know," she said.

"Aunt Hannah?" I asked. Hannah turned around and glared at me.

"And you as well. Especially you. What a wild vine you wish to become, Sarah Powell! Angie doesn't have to work hard to corrupt you. You're willing to dive right in with her because your father gave you a push off the deep end. You want to blame him for it, but it isn't all him. Worst of all, you're willing to take Robert with you, and Robert doesn't have the good sense to put the brakes on either. I don't want to spend the remaining years of my newfound freedom shackled to caring for my grandchildren's broken lives because their parents insisted on being stupid."

"And that's what you think we are?" I shot back.

"Prove me wrong, then. Be smart about what you're doing. Get one relationship working perfectly before you see if you want to add another. You and Robert barely know each other! Not even a year yet!"

Mom's words stung sharply, especially because she was right. She wasn't saying we couldn't have a threesome. She said we weren't ready for it yet.

"We can still date, right?" Robert asked nervously.

"Goodness, yes! I want you to date and get to know each other! But take it slow! Let Sarah put her own bra on for pity's sake."

Robert blushed. "You heard?"

Mom laughed. "Yes, I heard. I have a beautiful daughter. I don't fault you for being curious. Just be careful and patient. You'll know the right time. Or at least, that's what I tell myself. Now that I'm dating, I'm in the same boat as you."

Hannah was very quiet for several days after the funeral. Hers was a life built on rage. She hated her family. Grandpa's embracing her seemed to drain a lot of the poison from her system. Maybe that was as close to an apology as she was ever going to get from her father, but it clearly meant something to her. She and Mom talked a lot during that time. Mom never discussed what was said. Hannah would only say that my mother was developing the fine art of the velvet scold, a poetic way of telling you that you were full of shit while making you feel loved at the same time. She could be the still, small voice in the maelstrom of life, mimicking the supposed attributes of the God she still firmly believed in. I didn't know if I believed in God anymore, but the way Mom spoke brought me comfort.

***

Hannah's editor did read my story. Hannah and I sat together in front of the speakerphone as she shared her opinion.

"It's good," Tracy said. "Not to Hannah's standards, of course, but for a young woman of your age, it's outstanding. I have some concerns about certain aspects of it that we can address going forward, and it will need a lot of work to meet the standards we have for publishing here at Franklin and Hutchinson, but the higher-ups are willing to give you a shot. We're getting an offer put together to send to Erin, and we'll see where things go from there."

"What didn't you like?" I asked nervously.

"It gets a little preachy at times, dear. The story drags in spots, especially when you get lost in the arcane lore of the exorcist clans. Some of it is very explicit for a young adult novel! Good grief, where did you come up with some of those scenes?"

"A friend of mine helped me with those. She's seventeen and has an interesting life," I said wryly.

"Dear God, I should think so!"

"Young people these days are not quite so innocent as you might think, Tracy," Hannah said, giving me a smile. "The part about seducing her teacher is strictly fiction, though. That I can assure you."

"Thank heavens for small things," Tracy sighed. "We'll have a chat about that scene, I'm sure. But I think you're going to be a published author with this book once we work everything out. I hope it will be with our company." Erin and Chandra did work out the contract details. *Shadowfall* will be a real book sometime in the next year or so, once everything is completed. I can't wait!

***

School began, and life went back to normal. We had our daily study sessions. We went to football games to cheer Yuki on when she performed with the marching band at halftime. Robert asked me to the Homecoming Dance, and I said yes. Angie and Kelcee went together. Everyone had a date as well. Yuki was asked by a junior named Scott, something she took great pride in bragging about, even though none of us really cared.

Charli was one of the teachers picked to chaperone. She was younger than the other teachers and occasionally snuck out on the dance floor herself, lost in the music and the moment. Mom watched her from the sidelines, spellbound by her movements.

She was falling in love with her before my eyes, and I couldn't be happier.

After the dance ended, Robert and I decided to wait for Mom in the cafeteria while she and the other chaperones finished their duties and ensured everyone had left the building. We were talking when Angie and Kelcee walked in.

"You two headed out for the evening?"

Angie kissed Kelcee on the cheek. "We're staying over at her place tonight; otherwise, I'd give you two a lift home."

"We're going to call Joey before bed. He wanted to know how the dance went," Kelcee added.

"Glad to hear you're still talking," I said with a smile.

"So far, he hasn't found anybody to replace us yet." Kelcee had a wistful expression. Her mind was elsewhere. Angie noticed it, too.

I decided to try to smooth things over. "I didn't think he would. You three will be fine."

Angie pulled my chair out from under the table and promptly sat down on my lap, facing me. "You two aren't going to get in any trouble tonight, are you?

"I wish!" I laughed. "Doesn't mean we won't think about it. You're the ones getting in trouble. Tell me your adventures tomorrow."

"That's a deal. I promise not to leave anything out." She turned and smiled at Robert. "I might tell you, too, if you're good. Girl on girl is hot!"

Robert immediately found himself hiding behind a chair. "Tease!" he grumbled, though he was smiling as he said it.

Angie got up off my lap and went to reclaim Kelcee. "We're going to grab ice cream before we retire for the evening. See you tomorrow!" With that, they breezed off in search of adventure, leaving us in the cafeteria.

"Is that going to be us when we're seniors?" Robert asked.

"I don't know." I hugged Robert tightly. "Where will we be in two years? What's going to happen to us? Will there be an us? Or will there be a three?"

"Dunno. At the moment, there are two," Robert said. "One of us wants to kiss the other. Do you mind?"

"Not at all!" We kissed each other in the cafeteria, warmly and passionately, until we heard the door open and a familiar voice greeting us.

"No, no, no! Not in the cafeteria! What on earth are you two doing? Knock it off!" Charli was standing there scowling at us. Mom was behind her, trying not to laugh. "Take these two home before they get any further."

"You didn't mind when we did that the other day," Mom teased her.

"We weren't on school grounds," Charli said, cracking just the slightest hint of a smile.

"Come on, you two. Miss Reimer looks like she's about to issue five hundred words each on inappropriate lunchroom behavior. I'll tell your father you got caught canoodling by a teacher if you're not careful on the ride home."

"Yes, Ms. Powell," Robert said.

"Canoodling?" Charli asked incredulously. "Did you drive a horse and buggy here?"

"If you're going to date an older woman, you'll have to put up with a bit of old-fashioned language now and then. My grandmother was fond of that word, and my mother adopted it from her."

"Whatever. Drive safely. Call me when you get home." Charli hugged her.

"Now *you* sound like *my* mother!"

As we walked out to the car, Robert put his arm around me, and I nestled into his embrace. Yeah, this wasn't the same level of intimacy that Angie and Kelcee played at, but I felt comfortable here. I wasn't going to make it until my wedding night. Hell, making it until the end of high school seemed a tall order. On this night, I felt the ground under my feet supporting me, and I took a deep breath of the night air. The story of Sarah Powell, novelist, is only beginning. I can't wait to see what I become…

Book two of the Shadowfall Chronicles, *The Waters of Shadowfall,* will likely be released in 2027.